Shar[...] Jenkins 2008

# Bloody Money III

## The City Under Seige

### A novel by

### Leondrei Prince

Street Knowledge Publishing LLC
Website: www.streetknowledgepublishing.com
Myspace: www.myspace.com/streetknowledgepublishing

## Bloody Money III®

## Bloody Money III

Is a work of fiction. Any resemblance to real people, living or dead, actual events, establishments, organizations, or locales are intended to give the fiction a sense of reality and authenticity.  Other names, characters, places and incidents are either products of the author's imagination or are used fictitiously. Those fictionalized events & incidents that involve real persons did not occur and/ or be set in the future.

Published by: Street Knowledge Publishing
Written by: Leondrei Prince
Edited by: Dolly Lopez
Cover design by: Marion Designs/www.mariondesigns.com
Photos by: Marion Designs


For information contact:
Street Knowledge Publishing
P.O. Box 345
Wilmington, DE 19801
E-mail: jj@streetknowledgepublishing.com
Website: www.streetknowledgepublishing.com
Myspace: www.myspace.com/streetknowledgepublishing


ISBN-10: # 0-9799556-4-5
ISBN-13: # 978-0-9799556-4-8

# Acknowledgements

First, I want to say that Allah is Akbar. He's truly the Greatest God. I want to also say, Rest in Peace to my beautiful grandmother, Mrs. Beatrice "Gammy" Stevens, whom I wished the world would have had a chance to meet, because that way we'll all have had an opportunity in this life time to see and meet a real living angel.

I want to say to my brother and sister, Mr. Radee Prince and Ms. Rayya Prince, that I love you both to life, fuck death. We've experienced enough of that.

To my family, which is way too many to name, I love you all (the Redden's, the Grinages, the Brutons, the Owens, the Andersons, the Smiths and Williams), thanks for loving the craziest brother, nephew and cousin, y'all have…uncle too!

This book is for my fans. I love y'all. At last I've finally gotten all of the play up out of me. I'm ready to meet the people who support Leondrei Prince. Look forward to seeing me at book signings, book club meetings, etc.

To Diva's Dream Big Book Club, I sincerely apologize for missing that month last year, I owe y'all one. Whass'up Coast to Coast Readers? Hey, Raya and Lady Scorpio.

To my baby, my lust and my desire that I miss so bad. Let's just call her E&J. I'ma marry you one day, promise.

To my brother from another mother, my boy and still my best friend after all we went through. Mr. Joseph "Joe-Joe" Jones, I'm sorry for letting the streets mislead me and cause us to split. But we back, nigga, and we stronger than ever. It's ya boah. And my pen sets reigns supreme.

To my boahs, Dré Shelton and André Jones Hob, ya head niggaz. André "Breezer" Jones, the world will know who you are real soon. Gangsta Boogie, will be on shelves real soon.

To the ATL's #1 Underground Label, "The Trac Shac." Thanks for the soundtrack to the Bloody Money III Book…"Whass'up", "Ho Show", "Lil' Drizzle", "Young Cashus", "Big Dippa", "Numbers", and "Phoenix". The hottest bitch in the rap game, "The realest I know fo'sho.

To Block Ent., "Whass'up Block", "Big Dino", "Young Joc", "Boyz N Da 'Hood", it's your favorite author – Prince of the Pen. Donald Goines is da thing.

Cousin Dax and "De Boi Clothing" solo at "Trend" in the South Dekalb Mall…whass'up?

Now this is my most important shout out of'em all. This will be the realest shit I ever wrote. To the Urban World/Hip-Hop Fiction readers. See, there's a lot about Leondrei Prince that y'all don't know. If I told y'all, you still wouldn't be able to understand. See, I'm not a author at heart, I'm a street nigga. A hustla, a player, a gangsta and a pimp by blood. I'm not in no way glorifying any of those titles, it's just who I am. I couldn't help that, however, I can change that. But, if I hadn't been any of those things I said, I would not be the writer I am today. Experience is the best teacher. I think my pen bares witness to that. I am not a fake. My record is on file, you gotta computer.

This book is for all my niggaz out there grinding the hell out of these novels. Especially on the streets. My nigga, Brian, in West Philly 52nd and Market. My boy, Urban Anthony in North Philly, Spring Garden and Board. My nigga, Khalil in North Philly, much, much love and a huge big up goes to my big brother, Hakeim, owner of Black and Nobel Books and Distributions on Broad and Erie Avenue, keep distributing that work and playing the game fair. It's a lot of phonies, they know who they are.

iii

To my boy, Mussamba (Queens, New York), to Sidi 125th (Harlem, New York), and finally, to the hustlin'est nigga in the entire book game, my big uncle, Big Homie, and big brother, "The D.C. Bookman", Mr. Carvelus. As-Salaam-Alaikum. Playa, I love you man on some real shit.

To my real authors, Mr. Treasure Blue, Mr. Al-Sadiq Banks, Richard Jeanty, Kwan, Mark Anthony, Anthony Whyte, Vickie Stringer, Nikki Turner, Edna Jones, Ebony Stroman, Tony Nviez, whass good? My entire street knowledge publishing team.

To my Route 13, Route 40 split connection, shout out to all my ho's slash sisters, slash family, slash friends. It was y'all who had my back when I relapsed and made heroin my number one choice. It was y'all who had my back through all my down times. It was y'all that had my back when everybody, including my family, turned their back on me. It was y'all that loved me, helped me through my grandmother's death, and I have to let the world know who y'all are. I love you ho's like family. In fact, y'all are family.

To Monique a/k/a Mo Money $. My bottom bitch and my main girl. I love you, ho. And that's real shit. Don't let a mutha'fucka tell you anything different. It's true. Anytime a person can sacrifice their mind, body and soul, risk the chance of being killed, raped or beaten by some sick John or Date just to make sure "Daddy" is alright, deserves to be loved, appreciated and recognized, and no one does it like to Mo Money $. I love you.

To the rest of my babies on Cash Avenue a/k/a New Castle Avenue, I ain't forget about you ho's. Dawn M. L.L. Snow White, Aunt Karyn, Mirta a/k/a Da Spanish Mommy, Lindsey, Chyna Doll, Chrissy, Tuesday, February, Laney, Juana Brussel Sprouts, J-Hood, Patricia Aikins, Gina, Tina, Stephanie, Jenn, Slim, Ann Marie, Flame, Chasity, Blondie, Megan, Shelly a/k/a Shit Feet, Nineteen, Brianna, Cindee, Pooh Bear, Bobby, Lil' Nikki, Cousin Nikki, Cousin Crystal and her baby sister, Turk, Cee-Cee, and whoever else I missed, Daddy loves you too.

iv

To my celly's Ken-Cash and Donté "First" Dillard. Thanks for the insight. Had I not come back to jail, I probably would have never finished the book. My boy, Dave Ashton, Hold ya head! To cousin Nelson, stay up and stay focused. Jose Santos, Andres Rodriguez.

To my cousin, Pam Cooper and Black. Pinky and "Big Perdie", yeah, y'all thought I forgot y'all, huh? (Smiles), and Barbra Rosario.

To my daughters, Ms. Khalia Thomas and Key'aarah Prince, daddy loves y'all.

To my "Cousin 50) and (Twan Mega) Cousin Allison's knucklehead sons.

To the Delaware State Governor's Task Force, thanks for kicking in my doors at the motels almost every night, trying to stop the girls from working. Whass'up?

**I'm Out**

P.S. Ain't No Money Like Ho Money

P.S. Ms. McBribe over at Gander Hill Prison – thanks

# Chapter One

Today was the day that marked the second year anniversary of Tameeka's death. However, it also marked the birthday of their God's gift to one another, Little Tameeka, and just like last year, Rasul was on an emotional rollercoaster. Depressed and feeling lonely, almost angry at Tameeka for leaving him like this, but happy because every time he looked at Lil' Tameeka, he was reminded of the times...the times they shared. Even though her life was taken, the memories would stay forever...Like the day he was released from McKean Federal Prison. He would've never thought in a million years that that night at A Brave New World, he'd meet the girl with gray eyes.

"Why you keep staring at me?" she asked with attitude.

"Because I ain't never seen someone so dark wit' gray eyes before," he replied, and from that point on, they were one.

Like the time he blindfolded her and took her to their new home, only to watch her melt into his arms. Then there was the fondest memory of them all...The one where she strolled down the aisle on their wedding day, as Mosiq Soulchild sang Love. Now, all the memories get washed away every time he makes this turn from Route 13 into Gracelawn Memorial Cemetery.

Gracelawn Memorial Cemetery was one of the nicest resting places for the dead in Delaware. The other cemeteries were usually unkempt by the owners making it hard to locate loved ones beyond all the high grass and weeds. For Rasul though, it wasn't a problem...Tameeka had one of the largest headstones in the cemetery, making her resting place nearly visible from Route 13. Black Marble and Onyx trimmed in gold made up her stone. A beautiful portrait of her was engraved, followed by the words:

"Our Mother, Our Friend, My Wife"
Mrs. Tameeka M. Johnson
Sunrise                    Sunset
May 14, 1969                    April 11, 2004

Rasul pulled his Benz over to the side of the road that ran through the cemetery and got out. He made this trip over and over, but it never became any easier. Even now, as he stepped across the grass carrying a bundle of roses and orchards, he felt the tears begin to fall. When he reached Tameeka's tombstone, he dropped to one knee and neatly placed the flowers down around it. After that, he picked away any and every unnecessary weed and piece of grass around it, before speaking to Tameeka, something he did often.

"Damn, baby, it's been two whole years...and guess what? I still miss you the same as the day you left us. I pray for you all the time, and I continuously ask God for some closer. I just want to know why? How? And will I ever get to see you again? Well, baby, it's time for me to go. I gotta go get the stuff ready for the baby's party. Love ya," he said, then rose to his feet to leave.

When he reached his car, he looked back over his shoulder one last time before pulling off. Damn, he thought depressed.

■■■■■■

At the dollar store, Rasul grabbed a hand held shopping cart and filled it with birthday supplies. He grabbed everything from candles, balloons, happy birthday signs, party hats, hot dogs, potato chips, pretzels and tablecloths, all the way down to paper plates and napkins, before heading to the check out aisle. He was just about to fall in line, when this woman had caught his eye, actually stopped him dead in his tracks. She was the first woman he'd seen since Tameeka died that even caught his eye, let alone stop him in his tracks, so he had to say something. If only a simple hello.

Davita walked into the dollar store for a few quick items, that's why she left her car running out front. She only needed some more gauze, a bottle of bactine, and some tape for her shoulder wound that was nearly healed. The bullet that was shot from the gun her and Tommy was wrestling over had went straight through the front and out the back. She still couldn't believe she told the police that lie about what happened, instead of the truth. That way, his ass would be in jail. I guess that's why they say, love makes you do some crazy things. But Tommy Good was going to pay…Davita was going to make sure of it.

You reap what you sow mutha-fucka, she thought, and got madder every time she was reminded of what he done to her. Whether she was changing the gauze on her wound, or simply remembering her brother, revenge was on the forefront of her thoughts at all times, and right now was no different.

Davita gathered up her items and headed to the check out line, and that's when she felt his eyes...The ones that were glued to her back. She stopped to take a look over her shoulder, and made direct contact with Rasul's eyes, and her heart literally skipped a beat.

"Mmm...mmm...mmm! Damn, he's fine, she said to herself, and didn't realize her mouth was moving.

"You are too," he answered her, reading her lips. Then he flashed a smile only Denzel could make. "Can I speak to you for a moment?" he asked from across the store, and the two of them started towards one another.

"Yes?" Davita asked, when they were standing face to face.

"Hello, my name is Rasul. And yours?" he asked.

"Davita...Davita Good."

"Davita Good, huh? Any relation to Tommy Good?" he asked, and watched the glow on her face turn dull. "My fault, did I say some'um wrong?"

"No, you didn't say a thing wrong. And to answer your question, yes, Tommy's my husband."

"Lucky him."

"No, lucky you," she corrected him, not believing those words escaped her mouth.

"Is that so?"

"Yes it's so. Now come with me through this line before some juvenile delinquent steals my car."

"You left your car running?"

"Yeah. I would've only been a minute, hadn't I been stopped by you."

"Lucky me," he said, and they shared a laugh together. Just one of the many more they'd share together in the future.

■■■■■■

Outside of the Dollar General Store, Rasul and Davita's chat turned into an hour long conversation. They started off with the small talk. The how many kids do you have? The what type of work do you do? And the where do you see yourself in the next five years? All the way up to Davita's being shot, to Rasul's losing Tameeka. And before they knew it, they were both glassy eyed. They had heard of people hitting it off before, but it never happened to them before now. Right now they were experiencing what they had heard about through other people, and what they had heard was true. Everything people had told them about was happening to them. Right now, Rasul and Davita was tearing down walls and barriers that weren't supposed to be touched until some sort of foundation was laid, and they were doing it with ease. It was as if they knew each other for years, and were just now getting reacquainted with one another.

"I'll tell you what. What are you doing around 3:00 pm today?" Rasul asked.

"I'm not doing anything, why?" she asked.

"How about you and your two young ones come to my daughter's birthday party?"

"That sounds like a go."

"Good, then I'll see you then," Rasul said, then wrote his address down on a napkin.

"Yes you will," she answered, and they shared a brief embrace before departing. "You'll see us."

"I'm looking forward to it."

Rasul walked to his car and just sat behind the steering wheel for a minute. He was blank, almost felt like he had done something wrong. Like cheated on his wife or something, but there wasn't anymore wife. So why was he feeling this way? Then it hit him. It wasn't Tameeka that he was concerned about, it was Tommy...Tommy Good. The young cannon that claimed the streets when Rasul, Dog and Pretty E a took backseat. Rasul had heard a many of things about this Tommy character, but knew by the moves he made, he wouldn't last long in this game. From everything Rasul had gathered on the youngster, he found out that he was a live wire. Acted off of emotion not intellect. Didn't think before he reacted, and that could cost him his freedom or his life. His life if he decided to come at Rasul.

Rasul, Dog and Pretty E were the streets then, and still were now, even though they didn't play the game anymore. They had set the standard way back in the early millennium, and every youngster since was trying to copy their blueprint. Everybody wanted the lavish lifestyle Rasul, Dog and Pretty E was living. But was everyone willing to pay the cost to be the Boss? See, in the game, these mean and wicked streets, you're only going to go as far as your connect could take you. The only other way to succeed was by knocking off your connect and everybody else around you that was an interference. Then you had to realize that killing meant coming up. The funny thing was that it still hurt no matter what the amount the "come-up" was. And if this statement proved to be true, then wearing the king's crown or holding the boss title down wasn't meant for you. Only the cold-blooded wore those titles, and Rasul, Dog and Pretty E was as cold as they came. They had the brains though.

Tommy Good and Mike Cottman were cold-blooded too. That's why, right now, the streets was their's. They had managed to ""gorilla" their way to the top without a drop of remorse, and hadn't had any plans on stopping. Things were just a little hot right now on their end, you know, with the disappearances of Zy, Boomer and Peacock and all.

Then there was the bogus burglary report that Davita and Tommy made up that didn't line up at all. It had suspicion written all over it. So falling back was what Tommy and Mike had been doing. Trying to pick up the pieces and mend their marriage back together was Tommy's main focus, and how to end it was Davita.

# Chapter Two

"Tammy Washington, you have the right to remain silent. Anything you say or do can be held against you in the court of law. You have the right to an attorney. If one cannot be afforded, then one will be appointed to you. Do you understand these rights?" Detective Cohen asked, as he and officers of his department and Philadelphia Police Department raided Tammy and Pretty E's home that morning.

That was months ago, and she was still being held at Baylor Corrections for women awaiting trial.

"Girl;, you're going to be fine," Tammy's friend, Monique, said as the four horsewomen, as they were called, sat around the table playing spades.

"I already told her that, Mo. I don't know why she keep stressin'," Snow White, an ex-prostitute and drug addict said.

"Girl, you better look at your Rule 16, there is no way in the world you could've killed no damn Lucy! They just trying to hold you. Girl, the autopsy said that the victim's neck was broke by a bare hand, and the bruises on her neck came from the killer's hand. Girl, ain't no way your tiny fingers match those bruises on her neck. Girl, your shit ain't even going to trial," Chyna-Doll, another ex-prostitute and drug addict said.

Actually, all of the four horsewomen, besides Tammy, was ex-prostitutes…Monique, Snow White and Chyna-Doll. The crazy thing was that right now these bitches were at the top of their game. Wasn't a bitch out there on the streets that could stand next to these three bitches right now, and Tammy knew it. She had plans for these hoes. These hoes was about to get rich, she just had to keep them away from drugs. Like the old saying goes, "Ain't no money, like hoe money."

"You don't think I'm going to trial?" Tammy asked.

"Bitch, your case is getting dropped at your suppression hearing," Monique said, and Tammy felt much better.

It wasn't nothing in the world more comforting then some muthafucka's in the same situation as you, especially when you were locked up.

■■■■■■

Lil' Tameeka sat at the head of the table in front of her birthday cake, with the giant number 2 candle on it. She was dressed in a pink Baby Phat sweatsuit, with the sneakers to match. She looked like a miniature Tameeka, her mother. Her hair was done in four huge plats, with pink balls on the ends of them. The parts that separated them were so perfectly lined, that you could actually see the grease that moistened her scalp.

Rasul stood behind his lil' angel, and nearly melted away when the other kids around the table began to sing happy birthday.

The parents added their own little version when the kids were done, doing it Stevie Wonder style, but even that couldn't take away from Rasul's moment. It was one for the ages, as he watched his daughter scream, "Yea!" and clap her hands at the same time...something she learned in daycare.

Dog sat off to the side, away from the table, so he could get a good view to take pictures. Had he been anywhere else in the room, he wouldn't have been able to see everyone, due to the wheelchair he was now confined to, but he still managed. As for Pretty E, he was off to the back of the room, talking on his cell phone. It had been that way since Tammy went to jail. The phone had become his new best friend. It was the way that the two of them closed the gap between them, outside of the weekly visits he made.

Rasul looked around the room, and everything seemed picture perfect. The only thing that was missing was the presence of Hit-Man, Tameeka, Tammy and Frankie. That's where the dull spot was at. However, there was a new light that brightened up the room, and clearly took away some of the dullness. Her name was Davita, and her and Big Trina were hitting it off.

From the looks of it, it seemed to Rasul that Big Trina was more happy for him than he was that he had finally met somebody. She probably felt that way, because since the day Tameeka died, he hadn't talked to not another female. It seemed to them, his loved ones, Dog, Pretty E, Big Trina and Tammy, that he had built up a huge wall around hisself and wouldn't let anyone in. And to them, it seemed that he was doing more harm to himself this way. It was like he had stopped having a social life, and had become strictly business. He drowned himself in paperwork…from club Ballers, to every other business they had, clean down to the landscaping business. He had become a work-a-holic, and Davita was just what the doctor ordered. A woman to bring him back to life, at least a social life that is.

Rasul looked over to Big Trina to catch her attention. Once he did, he gave her the look like, "Do you got this?" and she nodded her head, "yes."

"Yeah, I got this," she said, meaning overseeing the party for him for a minute.

"Alright," he said, and then he began to feel that strong urge of depression overcoming him again, so he wanted to be alone.

Be alone just in case he wasn't strong enough to suppress the tears he felt welling up in his eyes, and he sure didn't want anyone to see him crying.

Dog looked to Pretty E when he noticed Rasul leaving the room, and shook his head. Pretty E did the same. They had seen that look on Rasul's face too many times, so they knew he was on the verge of breaking down. They were, however, impressed by his sense of taste when they saw Davita, and knew that at least their boy still knew how to pick'em.

"Man, dat bitch is sharp as hell," Pretty E said, then continued. "Looks like I seen her somewhere before."

"Nah, not me, I ain't never seen dat bitch," Dog replied.

"Oh, shit! I did see her before. In fact, I know just who she is…she's doctor feel good, that's what her patients call her. She's a foot and hand doctor that Tammy used to go see. She got her nickname from her patients. They said, 'whenever we leave here, we leave here feeling good' and Good was her last name."

"Good?"

"Oh shit, Dog, you know what? I think that's the boy Tommy Good's wife."

"For real?"

"Yeah, I'm for real. Look at her wedding ring," Pretty E said, and as if she could hear them talking, she slipped it off and dropped it in her purse.

■■■■■■

Rasul walked out into the living room and flopped down on the couch in front of the fireplace. Right above it sat the larger than life size portrait of Tameeka he had painted in Chicago by a young up and coming black artist named Darnell Woodson. Then he let his eyes rest there.

"Damn, baby. I wish you were here to see the baby," Rasul said, talking to the picture. Then he realized that she was indeed there in spirit, and looking down from heaven. "Damn, Tameeka, I just wish we could've gotten closer. Maybe then I'd know what to do. It's like I'm waiting on you to come back or some'em."

"Baby, don't do that, cause I'm gone," Tameeka said, startling Rasul. "Don't panic, baby, and don't be afraid. Just sit there and listen to me." She continued. "God has allowed us this opportunity."

She spoke, but Rasul was having a hard time comprehending. She was gone, yes, but right now she stood before him…right beneath her portrait, and in front of the fireplace, ghost like.

"Baby, is that you? How?" he asked, puzzled.

"Because, baby, God says, Be and it is. He has allowed us this moment together, thanks to your continuous prayers, and my constant asking. Baby, if I could've, I would've fought with every ounce of fight I had in my body to stay alive, but I didn't. I didn't, because no matter how much y'all loved me and needed me, God loved and needed me more. So who am I to even entertain the thought to question judgment, or the law of our God. Exactly, so I allowed the Angel's to whisk me away, and look I even earned my wings," she said with a smile, then turned around to show Rasul.

"So, He is real?"

"Baby, God is the realest! Who else could make this possible? Baby, I only came to assure you that I was alright. I'm not coming back because I'm no longer of flesh. Baby, keep on keepin' on. Love the kids, Jaquaan and Lil' Tameeka, and let me go. I'll be waiting for you in the after life. Now get over here and give me a hug, then get out there to that girl, Davita," Tameeka said, with a jealous grin on her face. And as soon as they were separating from their hug, Davita walked into the room.

"Are you okay? Is everything fine?" she asked Rasul.

"Yes, everything's fine," he said, then noticed a feather in between his fingers. "Everything's fine."

"Okay, well I'm out of here with Trina," she said. And right before she left the room, she looked up at the picture and said, "She was beautiful."

"Yes she was," he said, as she left the room.

Rasul looked up at the picture one more time, placed the feather in his wallet, then left the room. The portrait's eye winked.

■■■■■■

"This is Bell Atlantic with a collect call from Tammy, an inmate at the C. Deloris Baylor Correctional Facility for Women. To accept this call dial 5 now. To deny this call, just hang up or dial 7-7 to block any future calls." Pretty E listened to the animated machine, as he talked along with it. He hated the recording shit, but he had to let it play out or it would've hung Tammy up.

"Hey, baby," Pretty E answered the phone after pressing the number five.

"Hey, baby. What'chu doin'?" Tammy asked.

"Sitting here at Lil' Tameeka's birthday party."

"Aaawww!" she whined. "How does she look?"

"Just like her mom."

"I bet she do, wit' them same bright gray eyes on her little black behind."

"Yup, that's her. I just think Lil' Tameeka's are a little more noticeable than her mother's was."

"Ooooh! Let me talk to my baby. I know y'all took pictures, right?"

"You know we did. Dog was the photographer. So, if you get any pictures wit' the head chopped off, you know why."

"Fuck you, nigga! I heard dat," Dog butted in and Pretty E laughed.

"What he say, baby?" Tammy asked, hearing them laughing in the background.

"He told me fuck me."

"I know that's right, Dog," Tammy chuckled. "Now put my niece on the phone," she finished.

"Say hi Aunt Tammy," Pretty E said, holding the phone up to Lil' Tameeka' ear.

"Hi Auntie Tammy. Bye Auntie Tammy," she said and pushed the phone away from her ear. She was too focused on the birthday cake, and all the toys in front of her to talk right now.

"So, whass'up, boo?" Pretty E asked. "Is everything alright?"

"I'm fine. I just want to come home, that's all. Have you heard anything new?"

"O yeah, dat's right. The lawyer should be coming to see you tomorrow. You got court next week," he said. "You should be coming home," he said. Then the one minute warning sounded. "Baby, let's say our goodbyes now before the phone hangs us up and we get cut off," Pretty E said.

"Okay, then bye, baby. And I love you," Tammy said.

"And I love you too," Pretty E said, and they hung up the phones.

■■■■■■

Rasul came back through the kitchen door looking rejuvenated. They hadn't seen him this lively for two years…since Tameeka's death. But they liked what they saw. He bopped in the kitchen like his old self, walked straight over to Davita and lifted her off her feet. The gesture took her by surprise, but she felt like this was where she belonged, as Rasul cradled her in his arms like a baby. He spun around with her so his back was to the entire room, and then they kissed. And for the first time in a long time for the both of them, something actually felt right.

"Uhm-mmm!" Big Trina interrupted, then whispered, "Da kids."

"Oh, my bad. Whass'up y'all?" Rasul asked the kids. "Are y'all ready for some Elmo?" he said, knowing that would take the kids minds off of what they just saw, especially Davita's.

"Yeeeaaahhh!" the children screamed, and Rasul called on Elmo, who was really Kim, Dog's wife dressed in a costume they rented.

Elmo occupied the children long enough for Rasul to verbally introduce everyone to Davita, so that in itself was a good thing. However, there was still a whole slew of questions that Pretty E and Dog had for Rasul. The main one…what are you doing messing with Tommy Good's wife?

# Chapter Three

Unit seven was where Tammy and the rest of the four horsewomen were housed at. Monique was her roommate, so she at least had someone she could talk to when confined to her cell, and right now was no different. It was count time, the last one of the night, and Ms. Whitehurst, the burly looking guard made it plain.

"I said its count time, ladies and wanna be gentlemen! Now, y'all need to get to them cells before I take my time tomorrow letting y'all out," she threatened.

"Fuck you, bitch! We'll lock in when we get to our cell!" Snow White yelled across the tier. "It don't matter if you let us out or not, cause we still in jail."

"Yeah, but you'll be in jail inside of jail," Ms. Whitehurst assured.

"So what, bitch! Jail is jail, and I'll be damn if I let a bitch like you keep me on edge," Snow White said. "So, bitch, I'm taking my time."

"Snow White! Snow White! Bitch, come on," Chyna Doll yelled from their cell doorway. "Come on and lock in before the bitch give you a 24 lock up."

"Alright, girl, alright, here I come. I'm just tired of that Whitehurst bitch. I can't wait to see that bitch at a Wawa or some'em. I'ma split her wig clean to the white meat, you watch," Snow White said, and didn't a person who heard her believe her any less. They knew Snow White was about her work.

Tammy heard Whitehurst yell count time, but still had a body full of soap, so she closed her eyes, ducked her head under the spicket and rinsed off. Once she was done that, she hurriedly wrapped herself up in a towel, grabbed her clothes and quickly walked to her cell.

"Washington! Don't let it happen tomorrow!" Whitehurst stated plainly about Tammy's late shower.

"Alright, Whitehurst," Tammy said, and stepped inside her cell.

"Girl, you better be glad she ain't give you a 24," Monique said.

"I know, huh?"

"Huh?"

"Oh shit. Mo, can you hand me that lotion right there?" Tammy asked.

"Here," Monique said, and held it out to her.

No sooner than she reached out to grab it from her, Tammy's towel fell off her body, leaving her naked. She was so embarrassed that Monique actually noticed her skin turn flush red for a second. She reached down to pick up the towel for her. Tammy was reaching too, and the two of them bumped heads.

"Oooh, girl, my fault," Monique apologized.

"It's alright," Tammy said, but felt uneasy about the way Monique was looking at her.

Monique was her girl and everything, but Monique liked girls. I mean, when she was on the street, she dealt with nothing but "John's" or "Dates" as they were often called, but her preference was females. Monique was gay.

Monique felt Tammy's uneasiness as her eyes raped her body, but she couldn't help it. Tammy was just that gorgeous. From her huge round nipples, to her bald vagina, all but a landing strip Tammy was perfect. Her camel brown complexion and deep dark chocolate nipples nearly had Monique creaming in her panties, sho she had to say something.

"Tammy, have you ever fantasized about a lesbian relation before? With a white girl at that? Do you think white girls are attractive?" Monique asked, breaking the ice.

The questions themselves caught Tammy off guard. She had never really looked at color before, but had fantasized about having a woman caress her, and her caressing a woman.

But to not sound too awkward, Tammy said, "I don't know, I really never looked at color before, or a woman for that matter."

"Well, let me reframe it. Do you think I'm attractive?"

"Yeah, I think you're gorgeous. You almost look like Drew Barrymore."

"Oh, so now I'ma Charlie's Angel?"

"No, bitch, I'm just playing," Tammy said, with her back to Monique. "Hey Mo, could you put some lotion on my back?" she asked, but Monique took too long to answer, so she turned around. What she saw made her gasp...there stood Monique buck butterball naked.

"Mo, what are you..." she was trying to say, but Monique was too smooth. Her pointer finger had caught the word doing right on her lips.

"Shhhh," Monique hushed Tammy, and began to caress her body in all the right places.

What was confusing to Tammy was that Monique's tiny soft fingers actually felt good on her body.

"Mmmm," Tammy moaned, and Monique knew for sure that she had her.

Monique started out slow at first, but the more Tammy loosened up, the faster Monique moved. With a soft kiss on the neck and a hard squeeze of Tammy's ass, the two of them were making out. Their lips connected and their tongues intertwined into a world of bliss, and before Tammy knew it, she was spread eagle with Monique's head dove down in between her thighs.

"Oh shit!" Oooh shit!! Oooh shit, Mo! Girl, Oooh! Stop dat shit! Oooh, Mo!" Tammy panted, as Monique nearly licked the man in the boat out the boat, and into the canal.

"Yeah, you like dat shit, don't you, bitch?" Monique talked dirty to her.

"Yes, I like it! Damn right I like it! Eat dis pussy, bitch!" Tammy shouted, as the once smooth sex session turned beastly.

They yanked, pulled, tugged, twisted, bit, nibbled, and caressed each other into exactly for the next twenty-five minutes, using a toothbrush holder and summer sausage wrapped in clear plastic wrap, until they collapsed into each other's arms.

The next morning, to Tammy's surprise, she was being called for court. She and the other females going to 5th and King this morning were led down to Booking and Receiving to be shackled and cuffed for the ride. This was the part that Tammy hated the most. The degrading part, the part that made you feel like you was an animal or some shit. Then to top it all off, the guards woke you up at 4:30 in the morning, and you ain't have to be to court until 9 or 9:30.

Tammy boarded the white court van cuffed to an older white woman who had been in the papers for the last few weeks. Apparently she had been drunk driving and caused a vehicular homicide before fleeting the scene. Tammy knew the lady's face from the news and newspapers, but she still remained silent the whole ride to court.

Deep in thought, she realized just how much she missed Tameeka, Pretty E, and the rest of the gang. Then she switched her focus to Monique and the other horsewomen...Chyna and Snow White, the three white girls you couldn't tell didn't have no black up in them. And right after that, Tammy thought about how they were going to make out on the streets.

One thing was for sure though, Tammy was going to have a place for them to live and work when they touched down. In fact, she was already lining up business associates of Pretty E, Rasul and Dog's that she thought could pass as a surprise date. With Tammy's brain, and the four horsewomen's courage to make shit happen, Tammy knew that they could become the next Heidi Fleiss'.

■■■■■■

When the bailiff led Tammy into Courtroom 4C, the first thing she noticed was her support system...Pretty E, Rasul, Dog, Big Trina and Kim. She lit the room up with her smile, but she still looked a mess dressed in those prison clothes. Her hair looked a sight too, going back in two huge cornrows. And they didn't know what was on her feet, they looked like some Chinese slip ons or some shit.

Tammy took a seat next to her lawyer, Jonathan Malley, at the defense table, and he whispered something in her ear.

"All rise!" the bailiff ordered. "The Honorable Judge Leslie."

"You may be seated," the aged and frail looking white judge said.

Within a matter of minutes, the state was presenting their case against Tammy, using her prior assault first charge as a huge factor in this arrest. It appeared that the assault first on a Malika

Tillman in South Philadelphia years ago was motivated by jealousy, and that's what they were going off in this case of the Lucy killing. They had it all panned out. Tammy was a jealous girlfriend on a fit of range, who lost it and committed the same act she committed on Malika on Lucy. Only this time, the knifing was fatal. Lucy wasn't as Lucky as Malika, and their case was rested.

There was no murder weapon, no physical evidence of any sort to link her to the crime scene, and the brutal ness of the crime could hardly be stomached by any sane person, let alone a woman. And Tammy looked as sane as any person in the courtroom right now.

Tammy's attorney defended Tammy like a sudden death goalie defending a goal. He blocked, batted, swatted and caught everything the prosecution threw his way, but he dropped the bomb with the autopsy report. When Jonathan presented the judge with Tammy's fingerprints, then showed the bruises on Lucy's neck, the comparison was as far as the planet Pluto was to the sun. There was no way Tammy was this murderer, and the case was dropped just like that.

It was amazing to Tammy how fast her lawyer had gotten that over with. Now all she wondered was why it took them so long to get her to court. And to think I stayed there all these months for some fingerprints, she thought, nearly sick to her stomach.

"That's it," her lawyer said.

"That's it?" I'm free to go?" she asked Jonathan.

"Yes, you're free to go. But first you have to go back to the prison to be taken off the inmate housing list, pack your belongings, and say your goodbyes to some friends I'm sure you met during your stay."

The first person that popped into Tammy's mind was Monique. Her first and last gay lover, or was it? She swore up and down that she was strictly dickly, but a little clitly on the side couldn't do no harm. She cursed herself for that thought, but it didn't seem like a bad idea.

# Chapter Four

Davita made it a habit to take off her huge six carat wedding ring, and drop it in her purse whenever she was in the presence of Rasul. She did it out of respect for him, because she knew Rasul felt uneasy about sneaking around with another man's wife, especially when the other man was Tommy Good. That's what really had Davita attracted to Rasul, because he showed no fear for the man that was so feared.

"I ain't worried about dat nigga," Rasul would say, and Davita would snuggle up even closer to him.

"Yeah, Rasul is the one," she would tell herself all the time, because every other man she tried to date was scared off at the mention of the name Tommy Good.

Like regular, Rasul walked around his car to open Davita's door, something Tommy stopped doing long ago, and let her out. Their stop was in Landover, Maryland at a restaurant called Ocean's, a spot Davita used to frequent while in college at John Hopkins. It was a small but comfortable spot, almost a snug little joint, right off the eastern shore that served seafood, Davita's favorite.

The table was lit by a small flame that flickered on the end of the wick of the candle that sat in the center of the table. A soft breeze blew in off the ocean front through a cracked window that their table sat next to, making the mood perfect.

"Isn't this nice?" Davita asked, extending her arms out across the table with her palms up for him to grab.

"Yes, this is nice, but nice is an understatement. This is beautiful," he replied, saying exactly what Davita hoped he'd say.

He grabbed her hands in his, and for the first time in a long time, Davita felt appreciated and respected by a choice she had made.

The waitress walked out from beyond the kitchen doors, with the plates in her hands. When she set them down on the table in front of them, they looked picture perfect, as if they were taken out of a culinary arts book or magazine. The lobster tails were brick read, sitting on a huge leaf of lettuce, similar to a lily pad. The baked potatoes were split down the middle, oozing with sour cream and butter, and the steak and salads were prepared like a chef's television show. The meal itself almost looked too good to eat, but after a few Martini's and a half an hour later, they were patting the corners of their mouths with napkins.

"How was your meal? Did you like it?" Davita asked.

"The meal was blazin'. I damn near could taste some seaweed on my lobster," Rasul chuckled, and again they shared another laugh, one of many more to come.

■■■■■■

Tammy got back to the prison on the late court bus, even after being released hours, so she was pissed. It was almost seven o'clock when they got to Baylor Corrections, and she was tired, mad and frustrated, as were the other women who got caught up in the courthouse bullshit. They weren't taking anybody back until everyone was done, and the old bitch was what was holding them up.

Apparently, the old bitch wouldn't admit to the hit and run, blaming it on her doctor. The defense was blaming it on her doctor, claiming he over medicated the old woman, instead of her just admitting she was drunk. All Tammy wanted to do now was pack her shit and leave, go home to her king and lay next to him in their king sized bed.

Tammy got back to the Unit at seven o'clock on the dot, one hour before their eight o'clock count. Hanging her head on her chest, she decided to play a little game. Make believe something was wrong, and Chyna Doll was the first to see her coming.

Chyna Doll noticed her when she first entered the tier, so she went and notified the other horsewomen.

"Oh, my God girl, I hope it ain't as bad as it looks," Chyna Doll said to Snow White and Monique.

"Me either," Snow White added.

"Dat bitch is faking like a mutha-fucka!" Monique shouted across the Unit, causing Tammy to fight back a smile. "Bitch, I know you hear me!" Monique said again.

This time, Tammy couldn't hold it in. She lifted her head, her smile became visible, and she shouted at the top of her lungs, "Bitch, I'm going home!"

The whole Unit began to clap and cheer. The warmth that came off the echoes of the cheers was overwhelming, and Tammy broke down. It was finally over. It seemed as though the weight of the world was off her shoulders. The four horsewomen were right there to give her comfort with a warm group hug.

"Damn, I'ma miss you bitches," Tammy said.

"Not for long though. Bitch, we all come home next month," Chyna Doll said about her, Snow White and Monique.

They were all three co-defendants in their charge of receiving stolen property and drug paraphernalia. They all got ninety days. The "John" they had got the car from had reported it stolen, and they were pulled over and caught with crack stems.

"I'ma still miss y'all," Tammy insisted.

"We going to miss you too," Monique said. "Especially me," she wined, and Chyna Doll and Snow White caught it loud and clear. "I mean, with her being my roommate and all." Monique tried to clean it up, but it was useless, and Tammy knew it. They all shared a joke within itself and laughed one last time together until they'd meet again.

■■■■■■

Rasul pulled into his driveway at approximately 9:00 pm, and parked next to Davita's new G.T. Bentley Coupe, a pink one at that. It was an "I'm sorry" gift from Tommy, but she wasn't impressed.

Rasul let her out his car, and opened the door to her car so she could get in, but only after they shared a warm embrace and a quick peck on the lips, and even that felt good.

"Bye bye, baby. I'll see you tomorrow," Davita said, and started backing out the driveway.

Rasul stood at the top of the driveway, right beneath the garage doors and waved, as her rear lights disappeared down the street. The nanny seemed almost happy that Rasul was home, which was unusual. She usually didn't mind staying all night, but tonight was different…the police had locked up her husband for resisting arrest.

"What's his bail?" Rasul asked.

"Two hundred and fifty dollars," the nanny replied, and Rasul peeled it from his wallet.

"Go get'cha man, girl. Go get'cha man," Rasul teased.

"And you know I am," she said. "You got some mail too."

"Whose it from?"

"I think it's from Jaquaan," she said, putting a smile on Rasul's face.

Rasul walked over to the little television monitor to check on Lil' Tameeka, and she was sound asleep. He then grabbed the mail from off the kitchen counter, and grabbed the letter addressed "Dad" and smiled.

*Hey Dad,*

*Whass'up? I hope this letter gets home by my lil' sister's birthday so you can give her a kiss for me. If not, give her a kiss for me anyway. So, dad, what's been up with you? You got a girl yet, nigga? (Ha! Ha!) As for me, I'm chillin'. Just dropped 28 last night against U.S.C. Oh, but you already know that cause they plastered me on Sportcenter. (Smile) Anyway, just wrote to let you know a nigga loves you, and needs a couple dollars. Holla at'cha boah,*

> *Love,*
> *Your son*
> *Jaquaan Johnson*

*P.S. I know, wear a rubber, right? (Smile!)*

After reading the letter, Rasul grabbed the photo and smiled. Jaquaan was getting huge, real tall and lanky. He looked like his mom too, right up around the nose and mouth area. That's when Rasul, for the first time, actually felt like a proud father...to Jaquaan anyway. And even though Jaquaan never made Rasul feel like a step-dad, he knew in his heart that Jaquaan's father lived in Philly. And at times, he and Jameel talked on the phone about Jaquaan and his progress, but that still didn't change the fact of the matter...Jameel was Jaquaan's father.

"Love you too, son," Rasul spoke out loud after reading the letter. Then he made a mental note to mail some money down there to him at Texas A&M. At the same time as he completed his mental note, the phone rang.

"Whass'up nigga?" Rasul said, after looking at the caller I.D.

"Whass'up Boah?" Pretty E replied. "Ain't shit, 'bout to go pick up the wifey from da joint, that's all."

"Oh shit! I heard dat, nigga. What time she get out?" Rasul asked.

"In a couple minutes," Pretty E said.

"Oh, I thought she was going to have to wait until tomorrow. That's how I got it at the courthouse."

"Nah, she comes home tonight," Pretty E said.

"That's whass'up."

"Yo, whass'up wit' you though?" Pretty E asked.

"What'chu mean?" Rasul asked.

"I mean, why is you fuckin' wit' dat boah's wife? You know we gonna have to end up killin' that nigga."

"Nah, it ain't dat serious," Rasul said.

"Fuck it ain't! That young boah is a cannon."

"Nigga, I'ma cannon!"

"I ain't sayin' dat. I'm sayin' you just gotta watch dat nigga," Pretty E said.

- 33 -

"Nah, dat nigga betta watch his wife fo'sho be mines, nigga," Rasul said.

"I heard dat. Nigga, you know I'm wit'chu anyway, right or wrong. I just want you to be on point dat's all. It ain't really Tommy Good I'm worried about. It's dat nigga Mike Cottman, his boah from da ATL. Dat nigga is crazy! Reminds me of Hit-Man," Pretty E said.

"Fuck him too! I ain't thinking about none of them niggaz!"

"My nigga. Well, look, let me go cause I'm at the prison," Pretty E said.

"Tell my sista I said whass'up."

"You got dat."

"Alright then, good-bye," Rasul said.

"nah, it's never good-bye. It's I'll see you later," Pretty E corrected him.

"I heard dat."

# Chapter Five

Davita pulled into her driveway at nearly 10:00 pm, the latest she ever arrived home. But she didn't give a fuck. After what Tommy had done to her, she rarely gave a fuck about anything that had to do with him. She still wasn't going to reveal her hand though. Tommy was going to find out the hard way…come home and everything be gone.

As she sat in the driveway, she gave herself a once over. First she smelled her hands, then her forearms, then her shirt, checking for any of Rasul's soft scented cologne. She couldn't tell though, so she squirted herself in all those places with her own Melon & Cucumber Victoria's Secret perfume…the one that seemed to drive men crazy. Then, as she gathered herself, she looked up at her once happy home and dreaded even having to come back to it, but she did…her babies were there.

From the outside, the house still looked like a warm and loving home. Truth of the matter though was that it was cold and loveless. Had been that way since Yolanda told her what she witnessed the night of her brother, Hollywood's, murder.

Davita walked up the walkway to the house, and noticed that it was dark tonight. The only lights on was from the kitchen and the dining room, and they looked dim. She placed her key into the door, but before she could unlock it, it was coming open.

Standing on the other side was Tommy, dressed like a chef. His effort or attempt to impress his wife went completely unnoticed by him.

"Come on, baby, you could at least smile," he suggested, and she cracked one on the corner of her mouth. "Damn, baby, I want my wife back," he said, and stepped into her to hug her. He did that because he felt himself losing her by the minute.

Davita felt like spitting in his face, but again, she couldn't reveal her hand. So she reluctantly gave in, and was glad she did when she hugged him, because she noticed something...her ring was off.

Tommy led Davita into the dining room, where he had set the table for a candlelight dinner. He led her to her chair and slid it out for her to sit down, which she did. She sat her pocketbook on her lap when she scooted up.

As soon as Tommy went to the kitchen to get the food, she slid her hand into her pocketbook and put the ring back on. In the back of her mind, she couldn't wait to pawn it. When Tommy walked back in carrying the food, she couldn't wait to crush his world.

"I ain't hungry," she said, and got up from the table. Tommy's jaw nearly dropped to the floor as she disappeared around the corner.

The next thing he heard was her feet going up the steps.

Tommy felt like killing her. He was getting tired of kissing her ass, but he knew that's what he would have to do to win her over.

"Can you please fuck me tonight?" Davita asked him when he walked into their bedroom. The question caught him off guard. "Well?" she asked again.

"Yeah, baby, I can make love to you," he said.

"I don't want to be loved, I want to be fucked!" So fucked is what Tommy did to her that night.

"A smart bitch...I'ma fuck you alright," Tommy said in his mind, as he thrust deeper and deeper into his wife with every stroke.

Her screams and cries this night was strictly a self-fulfilling punishment she placed on herself for not being strong enough to leave him. She knew though that one day Rasul would make him scream just like she was screaming now, so she let out a scream of joy, "Yes mutha-fucka! Yes!" with evil intentions.

■■■■■■

The parking lot was nearly empty when Pretty E got there, but he did see someone standing in the prison entrance. As he got closer, he saw clearly who it was...Tammy, his fiancé. He sped up to the entrance walkway, and barely got the car in park before he was jumping out. He nearly tripped over the curb to the walkway as he ran towards Tammy, but he was still in motion. Nothing could stop this reunion now, nothing at all.

Tammy saw the headlights coming down the long prison roadway, and had a gut feeling it was Pretty E. To her intuition, she was dead right. So, as the car started to slow down, she dropped her bags and ran full speed out the entrance door. She almost started laughing when he tripped, then when he regained his footing, she jumped in the air to his awaiting arms. Tammy wrapped her legs around his waist, and kissed him passionately as he spun around in circles. The wait was over…she was back in the arms of her king.

■■■■■■

The letter reached the campus of Texas A&M just in time, because the University's basketball team was hours away from boarding a flight to the state of Washington. Their opponents were the Cougars of Washington State University. To Jaquaan, the game meant more than just a non-conference battle between two top twenty-five teams. It meant almost a guaranteed birth into the N.C.A.A. Tournament of sixty-four teams, and not the N.I.T.'s.

Jaquaan opened the letter that had the words: "Do Not Bend Or Fold" on the outside, so he knew pictures were enclosed. He grabbed the nice little stack of pictures and flicked through them, smiling from ear to ear. His little sister was growing like grass.

*Dear Son,*

*I received your letter a couple days ago, and yes, it made it on time for your sister's birthday. Your Aunt Tammy just beat her murder beef, and is coming home. And hell yeah, nigga, ya pop got a girl. That's her in the pictures. She's not really my girl yet, but we're close friends. I didn't know how much dough you needed cause you didn't say, but here's a few stacks.*

*Love ya,*
*Dad*

*P.S. Drop forty points, nigga, then you'll be doing something.*

Jaquaan was laughing at the forty points part and folding up the letter when his roommate and team's center, Troy, walked into the room.

"Whass'up Jay? Got Mail?" Troy asked.

"Yeah, pops sent a couple dollars, you know?" Jaquaan said.

"Who's in the pictures?" Troy asked, seeing the pictures in Jaquaan's hand.

"My lil' sister," Jaquaan said.

"Can I check'em out?" Troy asked. Jaquaan passed them to him, and he flicked through them slowly. "Is this your mom?" he asked.

"Nah, my mom died. I think it's my dad's new girl."

"Sorry to hear that, but goddamn, she's fine!" Troy said, looking at the woman in the picture.

"Tell me about it. You know how the saying goes, like father, like son," Jaquaan said, and pointed to a picture of his girlfriend, Janell. She was a college junior at cross state college, University of Texas, majoring in psychology.

"Yeah, yeah, yeah, nigga," Troy spoke nonchalantly. "Just come on so we can be ready to fly out with the rest of the team."

"Here I come, nigga," Jaquaan said, grabbing his headphones and CD player, before tucking the three thousand dollar money order in his jacket pocket.

He pressed the play button to the CD, and the sounds of Atlanta's hottest underground label, Trac Shac came exploding through the speakers, as the chorus to the strip club's favorite chanted: "Who is dat star posted by the bar, looking cool, shooting pool, cut like Steve Harvey."

■■■■■■

Davita was in her downtown office, getting ready for lunch, after finishing up with her last patient until two o'clock. She sat at her desk, thinking of her new friend Rasul, and listening to the radio, while staring out the window, watching time go by. Almost in a daze like, one of her favorite "oldies but goodies" came through the speakers, by way of WDAS FM, and assured her of her decision: "You, me, and he, what we going to do, baby?"

As the lyrics to the chorus sung, Davita thought, *I don't know about we, but I damn sure know about me. What I'm going to do is leave yo ass.* She was trying to give herself enough courage to do it. In her mind, she saw herself doing it over and over, but doing it in reality was a whole different story.

Suddenly, her office door came open, and there he stood with an arm full of roses, and that sweet soft scented cologne floated through the air.

"You ready to go?" Rasul asked.

"Yes, I'm ready," Davita said, but she was already gone…gone to the moon.

# Chapter Six

The very next morning, after a long night of love making, sex was the only thing on Tammy's mind. The four horsewomen, after continuous tales of their many escapades, had convinced Tammy into trusting the power of the pussy. Now the only thing left to do was put her plan into effect. She knew that prostitution was illegal in the State of Delaware, so an escort service was out of the picture. She had to figure out a way around it.

Damn, what can I do? she thought, and just like a light bulb clicking on in her head, a bright idea popped up. "That's it! I'm going to open up a massage parlor," she concluded, and went straight to work.

"Baby, guess what I came up with?" Tammy said to Pretty E, who was still sleep.

"Huh? What? Whass'up?" he asked, still more sleep then awake.

"Baby, get up," she pleaded. "Guess what I came up with?" she asked him again, after explaining to him all last night her plans.

"Baby, what? What you come up with?" he asked.

"A massage parlor," she said.

"A massage parlor?" he asked.

"Yeah, ain't that a great idea? Then the girls can sell pussy in the back, huh? Do that shit on the low."

"Damn, that shit do sound right," Pretty E said.

"Think it'll work?" she asked.

"Yeah, it'll work."

"Okay then. Oh, by the way, baby, can you buy me a building?" Tammy asked.

"I knew it was something." He smiled.

"Baby, you're the best," she said, and kissed his forehead.

"Whatever," he teased.

"Boy, you know you are," she said, and reached under the covers to grab his dick.

"Stop, girl!" he said, as he scooted away.

"Stop?" she questioned. "Oh, alright, it's like that. See if you get some more anytime soon," she said, and rolled over away from him.

"Sike, baby, sike. I'm only playin'," Pretty E pleaded.

"Oh, that's what I thought," she said, then thought, The power of the pussy!

■■■■■■

"That's why I love my husband," Tammy said to herself, after getting the call from Pretty E. It was barely lunch time, and already he had found a building. "Where is it at?" she asked.

"Baby, it's a blazin' location. It's right on the Market Street Mall, downtown Wilmington's Center City," he said.

"Damn, baby! For real?"

"Say I'm the best," Pretty E said.

"You da best," she said.

"Say I'm the best."

"You da best," she said again.

"Say I'm the best," Pretty E requested for the third time.

"You da best, daddy!" Tammy screamed.

You damn right!" he said.

"You so crazy," Tammy said, before hanging up. Then she started part two of her plan. She needed a business license, some parlor furniture, and some clientele.

After filling out the paper work, paying the $125.00 fee, and getting it notarized, Tammy had the business license. The business name was Relax Sinsations. She bopped up out of the State building, just as bright and gingerly as a hot tailed young teenage girl leaving her boyfriend's house. She had all kinds of plans for the massage parlor.

"My shit is going to be the hottest, sexiest spot in the city!" she told herself, before heading to furniture places and sex shops.

■■■■■■

"Is it the shoes?" one commentator, Clark Kellogg, said through his microphone as he commentated the game between Texas A&M and Washington State.

"No Clark, I doubt if it's the shoes. He's a diaper dandy baby. Yes baby, he's totally awesome with a capital 'A' baby! The super sophomore, baby! Hey big leagues, get ready, baby! Here he comes. He doesn't need to stay in school any longer, show him the money, baby!" Dick Viatel, colleges' best announcer said, as Jaquaan dropped his sixth straight bucket.

He was on a tear, displaying one of the single most impressive games since Glen "Big Dog" Robinson used to do it at Purdue.

"40 huh, that's all?" Jaquaan kept telling himself, when he dropped his 38th point of the night. "One more bucket, Pops," he said. Then it happened...the center, Big Troy, rebounded a jump shot by a Cougar guard, and threw a long outlet pass to Jaquaan on a break. "This is for you, Pops," Jaquaan said, and took off from the dots.

In mid-air, Jaquaan rocked the cradle and backwards two handed dunked the ball with authority. "Aaahhh!" he hollered, letting it be known whose night this was, as the student body section went berserk.

Then the yell of authority turned into the yell of agony when he landed. "Pop!" Jaquaan heard it sound, then the rip. No, he thought, reaching down for his knee as he rolled on his back. "No!" but when he lifted his leg, his fear was confirmed...his knee was gone. The entire sports world gasped.

■■■■■■

Rasul held the office door open so Davita could go out first. Then as the two of them left, with Davita carrying the dozen roses, Mike Cottman rode by. Mike was Tommy's right hand man.

"What?" he asked himself, not sure of what he saw. He knew it was Davita, but who was the man? Mike threw his blinker on, and floated across the street to a parking spot and waited for them to ride by. From his rearview mirror he watched the man open the car door for Davita, then he got a clear view…it was the boah, Rasul.

"What? What da fuck she doin' wit' dat has been ass nigga?" Mike asked himself, then followed the Benz when it rode by.

"Do you know him?" Rasul asked, noticing the car that had been following them since they left the office.

"Do I know who?" she asked, then pulled down her sun visor to look through the little mirror, to see who he was talking about.

"The car two cars back," he said.

Then Davita saw him. "Yeah, that's Mike, Tommy's friend," she said.

"So what'chu want me to do?" Rasul asked.

"Whatever you feel you need to do," she told Rasul, tired of snooping around.

"Alright," he said and pulled over.

Mike pulled over too the minute Rasul did. Like Rasul, he got out of his car, and the two approached each other.

"Is there any reason you should be following me?" Rasul asked Mike when they were face to face.

He noticed right away what Pretty E was talking about, Mike had the eyes of a dead man. They were dark and cold, and had no remorse or feeling in them at all. They looked like the life had been snatched from them years ago.

"Is there any reason you should be with my man's wife?" Mike asked coldly.

"Yes there is. We're actually going to lunch. Would you like to join us?" Rasul said.

"Nah, but I would like to warn you. Yo, make this y'alls last lunch," Mike said and walked away. "That's a promise," he said, before pulling off.

"Whatever, nigga," Rasul said, but Mike had already spoken, he wasn't trying to hear anything else Rasul had to say. He was in total violation, so anything other than "alright" was wrong.

So, as Mike pulled out to leave, he drove slowly pass Rasul's car and waved at Davita. She gave him the finger. She did that because she knew that he had something to do with Hollywood's death too. Mike laughed.

"What did he say?" Davita asked Rasul when he got back in the car.

"He ain't say shit. Was about to get fucked up, that's all," he answered, and Davita smiled. Then they shared a beautiful lunch together at the Olive Garden.

■■■■■■

When Mike walked through the door of his home, Ann was sitting in the living room watching TV. His mind was still occupied with what he encountered just moments ago, so he forgot to speak. No wonder my boy going through it, he thought. He was thinking about telling Tommy what he saw, but decided against it. He figured he'd take matters into his own hands.

"Are you going to speak?" Ann asked Mike, as he nearly walked pass her.

"Oh, my bad, baby. Hey, whass'up?" he said.

"Whass'up wit'chu? What's on your mind that was so important that you couldn't speak to me?" Ann asked. "And don't say nothing, because I know you, it's something on your mind."

For the next ten minutes or more, Mike explained to Ann about what he had encountered. He told her how he had run into Davita with some nigga named Rasul, on their way to lunch. And how Davita had gave him the finger. Her giving him the finger was not even an issue. Ann probably would have done the same thing to Tommy had he killed her brother.

She did, however, feel some kind of way though, because Davita and Hollywood were her cousins. The thing that caught her attention the most was the name Rasul. Rasul was the shit. He was then, and he still was now. Just the mention of his name made girls who knew him tremble. It wasn't just how sexy he was, it was the power and street credibility. Rasul was a living legend. She couldn't wait to call Davita and get all the juice.

## Chapter Seven

The Washington General, located in downtown Seattle, was where they took Jaquaan for his knee. The specialist wasn't in, and his knee was too swollen to thoroughly tell what the problem was. The doctor in charged called it a ACL tear until further evaluation, and threw his knee in an air cast.

Big Troy and the team's point guard, Kenny, was the only two that stayed behind. They stayed to support their boy in his time of what they knew would be depression, and smiled when he stepped off the elevator.

"Whass'up, baby boy?" Big Troy asked his roommate.

"They really don't know yet, but they scheduled me to see a specialist," he said, standing on crutches.

"Do they think it's real serious or career ending?" Kenny asked.

"They really don't know yet. Rehab will be definitely a must though," Jaquaan said.

"Yo, let's get your mind off of that. It's Saturday night, we're in the 'C.D.' (Central District) of Seattle, and it's a whole bunch of bitches…all nationalities," Big Troy said.

"Come on then, nigga. I need to get my mind off of this shit anyway. A nigga might even bump up on something strange tonight," Jaquaan said, and thought about the night Dog and Pretty E took him to the strippers on his sixteenth birthday.

■■■■■■

When you're from the 'hood, you usually like to get outside the 'hood to party. But tonight, Jaquaan, Big Troy and Kenny went to the debts of the 'hood. They found a little bar and lounge located in the C.D.

Club Dino's to the neighborhood was an eye-sore, due to all the crackheads and junkies that flooded the street behind it, and the alley alongside it. They did that because almost every drug dealer from there played pool there and lounged at the bar there.

Jaquaan stepped through the door first, followed by Big Troy and Kenny. They were all draped in A&M gear and looked like basketball players. After the normal pat down, they were in the club. When they walked in, Rich Boy was throwing some D's on, and killing the air. They instantly bobbed their heads, as they tried to cut through the crowd that was elbow to elbow. When they finally found a seat, they sat and observed how they did it in the North Western region.

The saying, "Your 'hood ain't no harder than mine" was absolutely true. Because right now, as the three of them sat in the slums of Seattle, Washington, they saw what they saw back east for Jaquaan, in Texas for Big Troy, and in Miami for Kenny…the hood. The only difference was the way they talked and dressed, because they acted like any other 'hood nigga or 'hood bitch…straight up ghetto.

They talked proper, real proper like a white professional would talk. The only difference was what came out of their mouths. Their vocabulary was nowhere near the level of a white professional. The words consisted of nigga, bitch, mutha-fuck, and everything else. It just sounded funny coming from black people who talked white.

Jaquaan was ears and eyes the entire night. What he came to find out was that the people here wore North Pole clothing, PePe, Levis, and shit like that. Not the usual Akademik, Polo, Rocawear, G-Unit, True Religion, Red Monkey, and shit like that.

Instead of, "Yo, dat shit is hot", or "Yo, dat shit is fly", the people in Seattle said, "Yo, dat shit is filthy". They called crack "soup", and they called an ounce of weed a "zip". The culture was different, because even the 'hood was clean in Seattle. That was probably because it rained seventy percent of the time. All in all though, Seattle was the shit in their own way.

It had gotten a little more crazy since Hurricane Katrina, because the people of Foemar had sent a slew of New Orleans out there, causing the crime rate to sky rocket.

"What'up, bro?" Got dat good," the boy with the Southern accent said. "So, whass'up, wordie? You want some or not?"

"Nah, we straight, my nigga," Jaquaan said.

"Alright then folk, the name is Trent. I'm from Nawlens," he said, and that explained his voice. Also my niggaz, 'bout deez hoes, I'm da man. Black, white, Chinese, Spanish, Ethiopian, whatever, nigga, I got dem hoes," Trent finished. Then he passed them a business card that read: "Anyway, Any Day, All Day – Ya Boy Trent Got Ass On Deny Way Avenue". And it listed his phone number. "Holla at a pimp," he said, and stepped off.

Jaquaan, Big Troy and Kenny looked at the card, then at each other and smiled. Their hotel was on Deny Way.

■■■■■■

"Bitch, you could've told me," Ann said, the moment Davita answered the phone.

"Told you what?" Davita asked.

"Bitch, told me about Rasul," Ann said.

"If you would've gave me some time, I would've told you. I didn't want to jump the gun, then have shit not work out. Feel me?"

"Bitch, well how is it workin' out? Did you fuck him? Cause, girl, he looks like he can fuck. I been wantin' to fuck him since I was a young girl. Bitch, all the bitches want to fuck Rasul, especially now since his wife died," Ann said.

"No, bitch, I didn't fuck him, not yet anyway. I plan on it though. And, as for the bitches who want him, it's a wrap. He's my baby now, and I'm his. I know you're calling me because Mike saw us yesterday, ain't you?" Davita said.

"Mmm-hum."

"I knew it. I just hope he don't go running his mouth to Tommy. At least not yet anyway."

"He's not. I told him to stay out of y'all's shit. We got enough problems of our own, you know?"

"I know that's right."

"Well, girl, I just called to be nosey, that's all. I'll talk to you later," Ann said.

"Alright, girl. I'll keep you posted," Davita said and hung up, then ran upstairs to shower. She had to meet Rasul down on the waterfront. Today's luncheon was at Joe's Crab Shack.

■■■■■■

Nearly a month had passed since the birth of the massage parlor, Relax Sinsations. Tammy looked around the once empty building with primer all over the walls, and smiled. It had come a hell of a long way. In fact, the spot was lavish…looked liked it could be on Miami Beach or Hollywood Boulevard.

Relax Sinsations was painted in a soft cream color. In the front lobby, there was three huge 150 gallon fish tanks placed in the walls. One held all colorful tropical fish, one held fresh water fish, and the other one held salt water fish, sharks, octopus and shit. Retro furniture furnished the lobby in all shapes and colors, making the room feel warm and relaxing, and the floors were waxed oak wood.

As you made your way through the establishment, the more exclusive it became. Plush carpet was the first thing you noticed, then the naked sculptures, paintings and designs. There were seven saunas and showers, seven individual booths, and four stations. The stations were for pedicure and manicure technicians. The seven individual booths were separated by dividers. Inside each one was an examination table with a hole cut out for your face to go while getting a massage. Chinese fans hung on the walls, and sex toys, wet wipes, hand sanitizers, condoms, towels, lotions, and anything else you would think of was in there.

Then there was a room marked private. The devilish room Monique inspired her to build. This was a dominatrix room. It was painted jet black, had black light bulbs, and a bed and swing inside. Leather whips, chains and handcuffs hung oddly on the walls, alongside of masks and costumes.

Tammy finished her walk through and smiled. The power of the pussy, she thought, before turning off the lights and locking the doors. *One more week before the grand opening*, she thought. *Just one more week.*

# Chapter Eight

"Yo! Come here for a minute," Tommy asked his wife, noticing something out of place. "Where's your ring at?"

Oh, my God, she thought, as she used her thumb to feel for it. "Damn!" she cursed herself, knowing where it was at…it was in her pocketbook. "It's in my pocketbook," she finally told him.

"Your pocketbook? Fuck it doin' in your pocketbook?" he asked.

"I had to perform a foot operation today at the office, so I took it off. Besides, I ain't want the mutha-fucka to turn green when it hit the water. It's probably fake as the mutha-fucka who gave it to me," she said, knowing her words stung him.

Tommy had hurt her deeply. This he knew, but Davita wasn't softening up at all. It seemed liked the more time that passed, the more distant she was becoming towards him, especially lately. It was like she had another man or something.

"Baby," he called out to her.

"What?" she snapped.

"Come here for a minute," he said. "Baby, listen," he began, "I don't know what I can do to make you believe me, but, baby, I'm for real. I didn't kill your brother. I told you before, when I pulled up to the house to meet him, it was already an inferno. The house was on fire. I was supposed to meet him there to cop," he said, watching how his words landed on Davita. They seemed to be cutting through her wall, so he continued. "Baby, Yolanda probably seen me leaving, that's all."

"Well, why didn't you tell me you were there? Why did it have to take for this for me to find out? That's the shit that makes you look guilty," Davita replied.

"I didn't want to be the one to break the news to you. I knew how close the two of you were," Tommy said.

"Bullshit! You did it mutha-fucka!" she said, and stormed off with revenge again on the forefront of her mind.

■■■■■■

This time they left the Texas Roadhouse Steak restaurant on Route 40. It was their fourth date together since Mike had warned Rasul about him being with Davita.

"Oh, so this nigga want to be hardheaded?" Mike asked himself, before pulling out behind them. Actually this time he didn't follow them, their routine had become so obvious that he just drove to the office and waited for them to pull up. And in a matter of minutes, there they came.

Davita went her way, and Rasul went his, with the "Hurst" tailing behind him. Only this time, Mike kept the black Celebrity with the limo tint, and the trunk full of dirt with two shovels way back. He didn't want Rasul to notice him this time.

Rasul had the radio playing softly as he rode. His mind was on Davita, and how good their bond was becoming. And his little mind was beginning to wonder how well they'd get along, as it pressed up against his jeans. For the past month and a half, they had really become inseparable. Davita was around him so much that it didn't seem that Tommy even existed, but that would all soon change. Mike was going to make sure of that.

Rasul got to Dog's house before kick off. It was the first game of the preseason, his Dallas Cowboys were playing Pretty E's Denver Broncos, and this afternoon Dog had to play host. In the beginning, Rasul and Pretty E had placed Dog on sort of a pitty-pot, feeling sorry for him, but now, as they watch how he maneuvered around in that wheelchair, they knew he was alright.

"What else you two niggaz need?" Dog asked, after bringing the beer.

"Where's the choke at nigga?" Pretty E spoke first.

"I know, nigga. Damn, what'chu, babysitting the weed again, nigga?" Rasul added.

"Nigga, the weed right there," Dog snapped, pointing to a candy dish on the coffee table in front of the couch they were sitting on.

"Oh shit, our bad," Rasul apologized. For the next three hours, they male bonded. The host next week was Pretty E.

■■■■■■

When Mike was set out to do something he didn't stop until it was done. So now, as he sat outside of this house, he again waited patiently. He saw the cars in the driveway with the license plates that read "Kim" on the Benz R 500. "Pretty 1" on the Maybach Coupe, and "H.P. 12163" on the G.S. 300. The other car was Rasul's.

"This gotta be either Pretty E's or Dog's house," Mike reasoned, as he waited. It wasn't until four o'clock, three hours later, that the front door opened up again.

Mike leaned up in his seat when the door opened, and grabbed his binoculars. He threw them up to his eyes, and was damn near in the living room as they came out. It was all three of the "has beens", as Mike called them. They were just standing out front of the house. A few minutes later, they were giving each other dap and handshakes, for what probably was going to be their good-byes. When Pretty E and Rasul backed out, he knew exactly whose house it was…it was Dog's, and *Oh, how sweet it is!* Mike thought and pulled off.

# Chapter Nine

The worst fear was confirmed, Jaquaan's basketball career was over, finished, just like that. A simple bad landing had cost him his dream, and millions of dollars. His tears hadn't stopped yet. Rasul didn't say anything to him as they left the specialist office. He had, however, planned on saying something when they got home.

40 points, 40 mutha-fuckin' points, Jaquaan thought. He thought about the letter, trying to come up with an excuse besides taking the blame himself. Because, in fact, the letter had nothing to do with what happened. He could've simply laid the ball up, but no, he had to get funky wit' it, and getting funky wit' it had cost him his career.

"Damn, Dad, what I'ma do now?" Jaquaan asked through sobs.

"Whatever you wanna do. Whatever you wanna do, son. I'm behind you 200 percent," Rasul said, and nothing he could of said would have made Jaquaan believe him anymore than he did now.

"Anything?" Jaquaan asked.

"Anything, baby boy," Rasul assured, and that planted the seed.

■■■■■■

Jaquaan took one step at a time to climb the stairs to his room. The specialist had him pissed off and angry at the world. It seemed to him that there was no way out right now, but he was going to do something. He had to do something, because living off his dad wasn't the ticket.

He pulled out his cell phone and went straight to his phone list to call Boog and O.D.B., Tish's lil' cousins.

"What'up, nigga?" Boog said, answering the phone on the first ring.

"What'up? What's good wit'chu?" Jaquaan asked, hearing his boy's voice for the first time in a long time.

"Ain't shit, baby boy. You know, still chasing them dead people," Boog replied.

"I heard dat. Looks like I might start chasing them wit'chu, feel me?"

"Hell no I don't feel you, nigga! You's a basketball player," Boog said.

"Was a basketball player. The specialist said it's over. I'll never again," Jaquaan said, and the phone went silent.

Boog almost cried. It was Jaquaan who him and O.D.B. was banking on to make it to the league. That way they could put the drugs down for a minute.

"Yo, you still there?" Jaquaan asked.

"Yeah, I'm here," Boog said. "That shit just fucked me up, that's all," he said.

"How you think I feel?" Jaquaan asked.

"I can imagine," Boog said.

"Where O.D.B. at?"

"Nigga just got out the Plummer House."

"The halfway house joint?"

"Yeah. Nigga tryin' to throw dick all around the city." Boog laughed.

"A nasty bastard," Jaquaan added with a laugh.

"So whass'up? What'chu trying to get into? You know it's two dollar Tuesday up Transit tonight," Boog said.

"That's a go," Jaquaan said.

"Alright, be ready around eleven o'clock. Me and O.D.B. coming to get you," Boog said, and they hung up.

# Chapter Ten

Outside C. Deloris Baylor Correctional Facility for Women was like de jevau for Tammy, as she sat and waited for the horsewomen. Today was the day that they'd be reunited. The day also marked the day that Tammy's idea would be put into effect. She didn't see any reason for them not to buy into the plan, because what else was they going to do? Yeah, they could go home with their families, because indeed they had families too. But how long would that last before they got bored, and ran back to the streets, started getting high, and working the streets again? Tammy got out of Pretty E's Maybach and sat on the hood.

Chyna Doll, Snow White and Monique were all called at the same time. "Bag and baggage," the guard called, after calling their government names, and they were headed out the door.

"See y'all!" they all yelled in unison, as they left the Unit.

The rest of the females returned the gesture. "See y'all and good luck!" they cheered.

Leaving out of the prison, they saw Tammy before they left the entrance. "Girl, look at Tammy," Snow White said, and they all saw her sitting on the car with three bags in her hands.

"What kind of car is that?" Monique asked.

"I don't know, bitch, but that shit is hot," Chyna Doll said.

"Ain't it," Monique and Snow White agreed.

Once they reached the entrance door, they did what they planned on doing, they looped each other's arms together, and like Lavern and Shirley, they leaped through the door together.

"Hey bitches!" Tammy yelled, when they came out the door.

"Hey bitch!" they said in unison.

"Now did you miss us?" Chyna Doll asked.

"Hell no! It seemed like we was together just yesterday," Tammy answered, and they all group hugged.

"You ain't even miss me?" Monique questioned.

"Oh hell yeah, you know I missed you," Tammy said, with a devilish grin. Oh my God, what am I saying? she thought to herself.

"You better had," Monique said.

"What's in the bags?" Snow White asked.

"Y'all clothes. Here, I got y'all whole new wardrobes," Tammy said. "This is just something for y'all right now."

"That's a bet. Tammy, thanks girl," Snow White said.

"Thanks for what?" Tammy asked.

"For being here. Having these clothes for us, and sending us money last month. You didn't have to do none of that," Snow White said.

"Bitch, that's what friends are for. Now come on y'all, let's talk over breakfast," Tammy said, as they loaded up in the Maybach to leave.

For the next two hours, Tammy, Snow White, Chyna Doll and Monique talked over breakfast about everything they could think about...from their days in prison to now, and the future. Tammy told them she had a surprise for them, but first she took them to their apartment she had leased right off of 273 and Route 7...The Christiana Meadows.

When Tammy passed them their keys, Snow White started to cry. She always did that. She did it while watching movies, watching the news, or hearing anything sad. She even cried when she was happy. So when Tammy passed her her key, she was overwhelmed with joy. Monique and Chyna Doll almost did the same when they looked at Snow White, but they didn't, they just let Tammy know how much they appreciated her.

"I mean, it's a little some'um. Y'all can do more as we go along, but all in all, it's right for now. Feel me?" Tammy said.

"Girl, we can't thank you enough," Chyna Doll said.

"Me either," Monique added.

The next thing they did after getting dolled up at home was glide past Relax Sinsations. Tammy gave them a play by play of the layout, and they each chose a booth, but Monique wanted what was behind the door marked private. They all laughed.

"Bitch, you is crazy," they said in unison.

"Nah, I ain't crazy, I just want to fuck some men up. And I'm fuckin' them up because their some nasty, sorry, perverted mutha-fuckas, who cheat on their wives," Monique insisted.

"You'll get a chance to use the room Mo, we all will," Chyna Doll said.

"When do we start?" Snow White asked.

"Next week. The grand opening is next week," Tammy answered, and they all left for dinner.

■■■■■■

The flyers and posters of the grand opening of the newest host spot in town, Relax Sinsations, was everywhere. Tammy, Monique, Snow White and Chyna Doll passed out and hung posters and flyers in all the barber shops, beauty saloons, nail shops, clothing stores, and at the corner stores they left stacks of flyers. They hung posters on nearly every pole in the 'hood. So, when Tammy opened the doors for business, the line was exceptionally long.

Monique, Snow White and Chyna Doll were dressed as sexy nurses, with fish net stockings, eight-inch heel stilettos. Their hair was pulled up into buns, and they wore imitation medical glasses on their faces, to give them a professional look. Tammy knew from the turn out today, that Relax Sinsations was going to be a smash hit.

For the next eight hours, Tammy booked and recorded down appointments of the men and business men who weren't able to stay today. They did, however, get a first class tour of the place and an eye full of the women who worked there, and was impressed by what they saw.

So, real professionally, Tammy smiled and kindly showed them to the door. "Okay, thanks for coming, and I'll see you then," she said.

Meanwhile, back in the booths, Chyna Doll, Snow White and Monique were working their fingers to death, as they massaged the day away. Only a few full body sessions took place privately, but all in all, it was a success. People, say hello to the newest hot spot in town...Relax Sinsations.

# Chapter Eleven

The rebuilding of a dynasty was what needed to happen in order for them to ever get back in power. So a few members from the original family contacted the other five major families, and the books were reopened. The Capelli family was back on the rise.

The tragic event that took place a couple years back had shocked the entire Italian community when Frankie and the rest of them perished in the fire, at the hands of the Moolies. The only thing now for the Capelli's to do was avenge their brothers death, and Rasul, Dog and Pretty E were at the top of their hit lists.

"I want his fuckin' head!" Franklin Capelli, the great grandson of Frankie Maraachi spoke to the new age Capelli's. "His fuckin' head!"

"No problem, boss, will do," Salvatore Capone, the under boss spoke. "Will do."

It was just that easy when dealing with LaCostra Nostra. You were just a phone call away from meeting your maker. That's where Rasul, Dog and Pretty E stood, one step away from their maker.

■■■■■■

Jaquaan called his stepfather into his bedroom to ask him the question. "Fuck it," he told himself. "He said anything."

However, Jaquaan knew better, Rasul didn't and wouldn't condone anything that couldn't or wouldn't benefit him in a positive way. So asking for this cocaine was a fifty-fifty chance. It wasn't a sure shot like anything else he'd asked for, but he had a plan against the answer no. He was going to use a guilt trip against Rasul.

"Whass'up, son?" Rasul asked, when he walked into Jaquaan's bedroom.

"I need to ask you some'em," Jaquaan said.

"I'm listening," Rasul said.

"Yo, Dad, remember when you said you was behind me 200%? And that you'll support me in anything I do?"

"Yeah, I remember."

"Well, look Pops, I've been talking to Boog and O.D.B., and you know they be out there on their grind. I'm sayin' whass'up? Put a nigga on. I'm a grown man now. I can't keep living off of you. I gotta earn my own keep," Jaquaan said.

Rasul knew it was coming. It was probably the single most difficult question he had to answer, but he was going to stick to his guns.

"Nah, Jaquaan, I can't do it, baby boy. I'm not putting no cocaine in your hands…anything but that. Your mom would roll over in her grave."

"She probably already did, knowing I broke my knee trying

to score 40 to impress you," Jaquaan said, striking out to hurt.

Rasul was speechless, the words he just heard had cut him deeply.

"Why'd you have to go there? Nigga, I'd do anything for you! But puttin' some poison in ya hand ain't cool! But, nigga, if that's what your young dumb stupid ass want, that's what you'll get. When your dumb ass want it?" Rasul snapped.

"Whenever," Jaquaan answered dumbfounded.

Later on though he'd apologize, but right now Rasul was mad, and Jaquaan wasn't going to fuck with him.

"Stupid nigga!" Rasul said, walking out the door.

■■■■■■

After the conversation with Jaquaan, Rasul was steaming. The nerve of that lil' nigga, Rasul thought, remembering the 40 point remark. "All I ever did for that lil' nigga was try and help his lil' punk ass." In reality, when Tameeka died, he coulda sent his ass up Philly with his dad, but he didn't, he allowed him to stay. So, for Jaquaan to say some shit like that to him was a slap in the face. He needed someone to talk to, so he called Davita.

"Hey, baby, can you talk?" Rasul asked Davita.

"Anytime you call I can talk, baby," Davita whined pleasingly.

"Where's your, you know?" he said, not even allowing the name husband or Tommy to roll off his lips.

"Not here, he went out somewhere. Why, whass'up?" she asked. "Are you alright?" she asked, sensing something was wrong with him.

"It's my son. You know that ever since he tore his knee up, he's been down in the dumps. Well, today the nigga asked me for some drugs."

"What?" she asked surprised.

"Yeah, dat nigga asked me for some cocaine."

"What did you say?"

"I said no at first," he said.

"What do you mean at first?" she asked.

"At first I told him no."

"Then you told him yes?"

"Yeah, what else was I supposed to do? If I didn't give it to him, he'd get it from somewhere else."

"Well, let him do that, baby. Cause if some'em happen to that boy behind you giving him something, you'll never forgive yourself," Davita said.

"Fuck it! I say if he wants to be grown, let dat nigga be grown," Rasul said, and for the first time since she'd know him, he had lost his composure.

"Baby, you mean that, do you?"

"Hell no I don't mean it."

"I know you didn't. Baby, think it over before you make a decision," she said, but he had already decided. He couldn't go back on his word now. "What are you doin'? Do you want some company this hour of the night?" she asked.

"Where's the kids at?" Rasul asked.

"Over Big Mom's…Tommy's grandmother," she said.

"You sure you can pull it off?" Rasul asked.

"As sure as my name is Davita," she said.

"Well, in that case, you ain't here yet?"

"Come get the door," she said, standing on his front step, naked under her over coat. Tonight was the night.

Davita couldn't believe that she had mustered up the courage to be so bold. Never in her wildest imagination would she had thought she'd be able to pull a stunt like this. This was way out of her character, but tonight she felt daring…horny for real. The last time she had had sex, it was more like a rape session, something she wanted inflicted on her self for being so weak and staying with her husband after what he had done. Tonight though, she wanted to make love, and Rasul was the remedy.

When Rasul opened the door to his huge Greenville home, he was almost shocked that Davita was on the other side. He had thought she meant open the door when she got there, but she was there now. And that was even more impressive to Rasul, because that meant as soon as she heard the distress in his voice, she was on the way to rescue him.

Standing there in a full length overcoat, Davita looked ravishing. Her skin tone matched the deer skin colored trench coat to a tee, and the way she had it tied tight at the waist, revealed her perfect figure. Rasul nearly drooled at the mouth.

It had been more than enough time, in fact, it was long overdue. Rasul should've gotten some pussy by now. However, pussy was the last thing on his mind. He had lost his wife two years ago...the only person who could satisfy him in that way. Matter of fact, his wife was the only one he wanted to satisfy him in that way. That's what separated Rasul from the rest of them. He would've waited forever if Tameeka hadn't came back to free him of the bondage he was in.

Rasul didn't say a word when he grabbed on to Davita, and passionately kissed her. Her soft pants and the smell of her breath coming through her nose, turned Rasul on to the extreme. He was barely able to keep his composure, but totally lost it when he began to unbutton Davita's coat. She was buck naked, and her kitty had drooled on her legs from the excitement.

Rasul bent down to pick her up, placing his arms in between her thighs before lifting, and there she sat. With her back against his forearms and shoulder blades on the palms of his hands, Davita let her legs swing over his shoulders, leaving her prize at mouth's length. Rasul handled his business.

With his tongue jabbing in and out of her slit, lips puckering up to suck on her clit, and hands constantly caressing her back and ass, Davita went haywire. She didn't know what to do...grab his head, pull his ears, or snatch her own damn hair out.

But she had to do something or she'd go crazy, so she did the next best thing, screamed at the top of her lungs.

"Oh my God!" she yelled, and exploded into Rasul's mouth.

Rasul's dick was harder than a fucked up Rubik Cube was to fix, as he carried Davita to his bedroom. He laid her down on his bed, and started to ease his way on top of her, but she stopped him. She grabbed his dick, wanting to taste him, but he stopped her. Getting some head was the last thing on his mind, feeling her insides was almost a dying need.

"Mmm-uhm, baby, later for that. I want to feel you," he said, and that's what he did. He felt her…every nook and cranny of her until he was panting and out of breath. And like Regina Belle sang, Rasul was in love under new management too.

# Chapter Twelve

Relax Sinsations had taken in more income this month than Tammy could have ever imagined taking in, especially by only having three booths occupied. So, she hired some young nail technicians to work the manicure and pedicure stations, picking up more of an income. What she had to do now was get more ho's, at least four more to occupy the empty stations. Because she had to figure that by Monique, Chyna Doll and Snow White averaging at least twelve full body jobs at $75.00 for the massage, $150.00 for some pussy, and $50.00 for some head, that was $3,300.00 a piece. Now times that by seven, oh, then times that by six days a week, now that's money. So, Tammy was on a mission. Besides, she didn't want to wear Monique, Snow White and Chyna Doll out.

So, to show her appreciation to them for a more than profitable month, outside sat three new 2007 325 BMWs convertibles, freshly delivered from the dealership. On Snow White's license plate read: Relax. On Chyna Doll's, it read: Sin, and on Monique's, it read: Sations. So how they were parked outside, they spelled the name of the parlor…Relax Sinsations.

When they finally calmed down, and Snow White had stop crying about the gifts Tammy had gotten them, she was ready for the meeting.

"Look y'all," Tammy began, as she sat at the head of the office table. "In a measly month and a couple of days, y'all have managed to open bank accounts and stack them up. Each of y'all have moved into y'all own apartments, which will turn into condo's at the rate y'all are going. And y'all have brand new cars, all of that in like I said, a month and a couple of days. So, to show y'all my gratitude and appreciation, not to mention my love for y'all, I'm asking y'all to come into partnership with me. That way, I won't feel like the boss, and no hard feelings should get developed. This would be, and will be our business, and there's no 'I' in 'Our', feel me?" Tammy said, sliding the contracts over to each of them to read, and Snow White started crying again.

"We feel you," Chyna Doll spoke for the three of them. "Don't we?" she asked Monique and Snow White, and they nodded their heads.

"So now," Tammy began, "the only thing is thoughts on how to improve the business."

"We need more girls," Snow White spoke first.

"We do, cause if we get them other four booths open, it would be on and poppin'," Monique said, singing the words, On and Poppin' like Chris Brown.

"Damn right it would," Chyna Doll added.

"Where are there some more at y'all know?" Tammy asked.

And they all answered, "Down the Route 13, Route 40 split," and chuckled under their breath.

"Who's going down there?" Monique asked. "Cause I'm not. I'm not strong enough yet to go into the depths of the 13-40 split. Let alone, the Glenn Hotel, the Fairwinds, the West, the Dutch Inn, the Super 8, the Relax Inn, the Super Lodge, the Rodeway, the Fairview, the Crown, and especially not the Hollywood. I got too many stories about the Hollywood, that's a book in itself," she finished.

"Me either," Snow White added. "Remember the Red Rose and Lafayette. Bitch, what if that was still up and jumpin'."

"Bitch, we'd probably be dead," Monique said.

"Well, bitch, I'm strong enough to go," Chyna Doll said.

"You sure?" they all asked in unison.

"Does a bear shit in the woods, and wipe his ass with a fluffy white rabbit?" she said, using one of Lee-Mudd's and Joe-Joe's favorite sayings.

"Damn right they do," they laughed.

"Well, I'ma be alright then," Chyna Doll assured them. "I'ma be alright," she said again, only this time, trying to convince herself. Damn, one small crack attack, and it's over, she thought. I'm off to the races.

■■■■■■

The Route 13 and Route 40 split were located in New Castle, Delaware. They were fast alternate routes, that if driven, could take you to the beaches of Delaware, Rehoboth or Dewy, or the ones in Maryland...mainly Ocean City. The other could take you to Virginia. It was a frequently used road, well roads for that sake, and it was a known spot for prostitution...a "ho stroll" as they called it.

For Johns, it was a place they knew they could get some strange pussy or a blow job, even something to get high with. And for the prostitutes, it was a source of income, a way of life...one to feed their addictions and take care of themselves. It also was a nightmare waiting to happen. Onc they never knew until it was too late, and they were raped or beaten by some sick predator, or ripped off for their money when they jumped in some car. That's why they stayed strapped with some sort of gadget or device for protection. And they were reminded to do so every time they thought about the pass and a guy named Steve Pennell, and his work van.

Chyna Doll drove her new 2007 BMW on this sunny day with the top back for the world to see. Letting her hair blow back in the wind, while her Chanel frames block the sun, she waved at everyone she knew. She had even seen some of her new clients from Relax Sinsations with their wife and kids, and flashed them a smile. Looking exotic, like from an island or something, Chyna Doll was shining on this summer day.

She rode the 13-40 split for nearly an hour straight, looking to see if she saw any of her old homies, while gaining enough courage to stop at one or any of the hotels or motels alongside the roads that she used to frequent.

Chyna Doll pulled into the new Wawa that stood where the old Red Rose Inn used to stand and parked by the pumps. She was blasting her music as loud as she could, and taking on admirers, while she fixed her hair to get out. It was unusually hot today, in the high 90s, so she was dressed in next to nothing as she slid her credit card into the gas pump. She heard the few barks and whistles as her car drunk the gas. Then to cause more of a scene, she bent over as if to tie her sneaker, revealing nearly her entire ass in the Daisy Dukes she wore. The barks turned into a wolf pack of barks and growls from the men.

She smiled, job well done. As they began to approach her, she lowered her Chanel frames on the bridge of her nose, looked at the men seductively, and started passing out business cards: "Chyna Doll, The Masseuse at Relax Sinsations. Cell Phone 302-543-1716, Business 302-571-1000".

"Oh, so you're a masseuse, huh?" one of the men asked.

"Yes", she spoke in her sexiest voice. "I work at Relax Sinsations, the new parlor in the Market Street Mall."

"I heard of that joint," another one said.

"So what do ya'll do there?" the first man asked.

"We do pedicures, manicures and full-body massages," Chyna answered.

"Anything else?" the second man asked.

"If you money is right, you can get what ever it is you want," she said, and kind of caressed her breast just enough to start up the men's sexual minds.

"Is that so?"

"You got my card. Call me," she said and sashayed away with enough switch in her walk to make the men grab at their crotches. She looked back over her shoulder and smiled, then thought, *The power of pussy!*

Chyna was just about ready to give up her search for her girls and call it a day. But just as soon as she was about to step in the Wawa's door, she let her eyes roam over to the back alley that ran from the start of Wawa, all the way down and into the back of Save-A-Lot Shopping Center, and saw her girl, Flame.

"Flame! Flame! Bitch, is dat you?" Chyna yelled from the top of her lungs.

"Chyna! Oh my God, girl! Is dat you?" Flame yelled back, and the two ran towards each other and embraced in the parking lot.

"Oh my God, girl! When did you get out?" Flame asked.

"Girl, I been out. I been out for about six or seven months. How you been? You look good," Chyna said.

"Bitch, stop lying. I look like shit."

"No you don't. You look like you need some sleep though."

"I do, bitch. I been up for three days."

"Are you hungry?"

"Yes, girl, and I'm broke as hell. I ain't had a date all day."

"Well, come on," Chyna said, and they went into the store and ordered two meatball subs.

"Where's the rest of the crew at?" Chyna asked.

"Down Tremont at Bald Head John's room with Blondie," Flame answered.

"Who else is down there?"

"Slim, Crystal, Blondie and Nikki. Mirda was there earlier. I think she left though. Her, Salima and Gina."

"Alright, let's go," China said after they got their food.

■■■■■■

The Tremont Motel on Route 13 was located next to Hatfield's Seafood and the Dunkin' Donuts restaurant. The horseshoe shaped motel was operated by an old fat white lady with a racist attitude, whose main focus was to fuck with people, especially black men and white women, because she swore to death they were pimps and ho's, and not a couple. She made it her duty to fuck with them the most, because she hated the fact that her own kind could be so naïve to sell their bodies to niggers. That just fucked her up. All in all though, everyone simply said, "fuck her", and did their own thing.

Chyna Doll and Flame pulled up in front of Room 12, music still blasting Sierra's new single, and parked. The first thing they did was look to the window, and like regular, the curtain pulled back. Next the door came plying open, and out popped Slim.

"Hey, bitch!" Slim snapped with excitement, when she saw her girl Chyna Doll. She looked back through the room's door, and said, "Come here, y'all look what the sun sprouted up."

Crystal, Nikki and Blondie came to see what Slim was so excited about, and they too went crazy when they saw Chyna Doll. To her, it seemed as if she had never left the old gang. Seeing them all together felt just like old times. She was back with her crew, the ones who rarely dated...Crystal, Nikki, Blondie, Flame and Chyna Doll, who would rather stick a knife or a gun to a John's neck before they'd suck or fuck them. Sucking and fucking to them was a last resort. They'd only done that when their life woes called for them to do so.

Now, as Chyna Doll stood before her old gang, she knew tonight would be a long one. Walking into the room was like walking into a time zone of the past for Chyna Doll. The room still had that cheap, stale disinfectant type of smell with the crack and cheap perfume mixed in, lingering in the air.

Chyna Doll sat down at the table, and right before her sat s stem, a pusher, and a big ball of Chore Boy. Her stomach turned instantly. Being around Tammy, Snow White and Monique for the last six to seven months, shc had managed to keep crack off of her mind. But now, as she sat together amongst old friends, she cursed herself for convincing herself that she too indeed wanted a swerve.

"Here, Slim, let me see your apparatus," Chyna Doll said, holding the rock that Crystal handed her in her palm.

"Here, bitch, and don't burn my shit up. And you better not push my shit," Slim said, passing her her glass stem.

Chyna Doll placed the glass stem with the Chore Boy smashed in the end of it in her mouth, dropped the rock, then flicked her bic. The sizzle that the fire caused when it touched the rock, sent her on her way. Chyna Doll was back, not the beautiful Chyna Doll that she had been for the past six to seven months, but the old one. The Chyna Doll that didn't give a fuck about nothing.

For the next five minutes, Chyna Doll sat completely silent. Then it happened, she had her first crack attack, and it was a severe one. The talk about work and getting them into the massage parlor could wait for now. The talk about who had some more rock was the topic now.

"Who got coke?" Chyna Doll asked.

"The boy on Vandever Avenue," Blondie said.

"Well, let's go," Chyna Doll said.

"Come on, I'll ride," Slim said, and the rest of them stayed back to get dressed and ready for the Ho-Stroll.

*Only for tonight*, Chyna Doll told herself. *Only for tonight.*

## Chapter Thirteen

Davita couldn't believe that she allowed herself to fall asleep last night. But after busting a nut like that, who could've stayed awake? Let alone, drive home from a bed that they already was laid up comfortable at. So, when she felt the heat from the sun's rays land upon her face, she jumped straight up. She grabbed her phone from her purse, and saw the eighteen missed calls, fourteen from Tommy. She woke all the way up.

"Oh shit!" She wasn't shook about staying out, she was shook because she didn't want to expose her hand. "Shit!" Davita said, and called her office. "Hello. Hey Pam, whass'up? Did anybody call?" she spoke to her secretary. "Look, cancel all my appointment up to one o'clock. I'll be in by then," she said, and hung up the phone. Damn, I ain't got no clothes, she thought to herself, and leaped from the bed, while Rasul stayed asleep.

She walked over to the closet, looking for a pair of sweatpants of Rasul's, but to her surprise, there was a whole rack of Tameeka's clothes. She hesitated at first, but grabbed a sweatsuit of Tameeka's, which was a perfect fit.

"I'm only wearing it to the mall," she told herself, not really wanting to wear it, but she had no choice.

Davita grabbed a piece of notebook paper, and her eyeliner and began:

*Baby,*

*I had to rush out because I was running late. I hope you don't get mad, but I had to put on one of Tameeka's sweatsuits. Remember, I came over here buck naked. I'll bring it back later on tonight when I come over. Thanks for last night, I love it!*

*Talk to you later,*

*Love,*
*Davita*

She wrote and sealed it with a kiss. The red lipstick stuck to the paper perfectly. She stuck it to the dresser mirror and was gone.

■■■■■■

Tommy paced the floor all night long last night and most of the morning, calling Davita's phone. He finally gave up after the fourteenth straight call, then called Mike to dump his frustration on.

"It gotta be another mutha-fucka," he snapped on the phone, but Mike stayed calm.

"Nah, I don't think it's another nigga, cuz," Mike lied. "I think she's just hurt, that's all."

"Hurt? Does hurt mean stay out all night? I swear to God, if it's another nigga, I'ma kill dat bitch! The nigga too," Tommy promised.

"Just relax, cousin. Go to sleep, nigga. Everything is going to be a'ight," Mike assured him before hanging up.

And here Mike sat since that phone call last night. Right in front, but down the street from Rasul's house, waiting patiently for Davita to emerge.

Davita didn't come out of Rasul's house until the next day around noon time. That's when he decided to do what he had conjured up the first time he saw Davita and Rasul together. Dog was a dead man.

He turned the ignition to the Hurst and pulled off, but only after he left a message on Rasul's phone. "Rasul, whass'up, folk?" Mike began. "See, you think you untouchable, you has been ass nigga. So, since you can't stop seeing my bro's wife, I'ma put some chink in yo' armor, fuck boy," Mike spoke, in his southern accent. "Nigga, what rolls on four wheels, and doesn't have a motor? That's the thing to go, next will be you. So, let me go, I'm fittin' to go handle that now, fuck boy." And Mike hung up the phone.

■■■■■■

When Rasul woke up, Davita had already left. He looked at his phone on the nightstand, and noticed the voice mail light lit up. He was about to call his voice mail box to check his messages, but saved them all when he noticed the letter and huge lip prints hanging on the dresser mirror. If he knew that time was limited, he would have checked his messages, and maybe would have been able to stop what was about to happen that would scar his life forever. However, the letter was more important, the messages would have to wait for now.

■■■■■■

The sky was turning from dark to dawn. The street lights were coming on, and the neighborhood was falling asleep when Mike pulled up to Dog's house. He felt good, knowing that Dog wasn't home yet. So he didn't have to play the waiting game. He would just run up on him in the driveway when he pulled up, and do him in then.

Dog turned into the driveway and noticed that he had beaten Kim and the kids home. Damn, he thought, knowing tonight he wouldn't receive his normal help. He would have to do it himself. Using the gear shift and pedal hook up that was specially made for the handicap, Dog put his Lexus in park. In the passenger seat sat his wheelchair, which he reached over and grabbed. He opened the driver side door and placed the wheelchair outside and opened it up. Then, using his upper body strength, he pulled himself from the car into the chair. Once he was seated, he leaned over forward and strapped his legs into the leg strap connected to the foot pegs. He hit the locks on his key ring to lock the car doors, and began wheeling himself up to the front door, not knowing he was being stalked by a lunatic.

From the moment Dog got out of his car, Mike was on him. He crept up into the driveway, almost cat like, and grabbed the handles on the back of Dog's wheelchair.

"Whass'up, Dog?" Mike said, in his deep southern accent.

"What? Who da fuck is you, nigga? And why da fuck is you holding my chair?" Dog snapped.

"Damn, right hostile, folk. Specially for a nigga helpless as you," Mike said, then it hit him like a ton of bricks. This was Mike Cottman, Tommy Good's right had man, and from what he knew of him, he was a cold blooded nigga, a stone cold killer to be exact.

"Yo, I ain't got nuffin' to do wit' Rasul and Davita," Dog said, knowing already what this was all about.

"Neither does Tommy, but Rasul and Davita are making him feel like he does. So, to even things out, I'm 'bout to make dat nigga, Rasul, hurt just like Tommy, cause I'm fittin' to blow yo Goddamn brains out, big bro," Mike said.

"No please!" Dog cried, as he pleaded for his life. "Please, my man, I got a family," he said, and Mike was tipping over his wheelchair.

"Tommy does too," Mike said.

Dog fell face first in his front lawn. His legs were still strapped into the chair, so it was a struggle to even crawl. Mike kicked him up the ass with all his might, making the act even that much more disrespectful. Dog looked up at his stalker and shivered when he looked into Mike's eyes, because his eyes looked like those of a dead man's...coal black. The wheelchair drug behind him, pulling up grass as he crawled away, trying to get away.

"This bitch ass nigga," Dog said to himself. If only I could walk, he thought, as tears began to well up in his eyes. Then they began to fall as Mike stood over top of him and pulled out his dick.

"Mix this in with your punk ass tears, fuck boy," Mike told him, and began pissing in Dog's face. He laughed in a sick way, as Dog spit piss away from his lips. Then Mike raised his .45, and two shells exploded like M-80 fireworks into Dog's face and throat. He never felt a thing, and just like he came, he left. Mike was never seen.

■■■■■■

Rasul was just finishing Lil' Tameeka's bath, and was putting her into bed when he decided to check his voice mail messages. The first couple was from Davita, explaining to him what a wonderful time she had last night. The next one was from Pretty E, telling him that he got word of some middle aged white boys or Italians had been riding around through the sets, asking about their whereabouts.

"It probably was some M.O.B. cats. I knew that shit wasn't going to be over just like that," Pretty E said. But it wasn't just some M.O.B. cats, it was the Capelli family reincarnated.

The last message though was confusing and real eerie. It was Mike, he could tell by the heavy accented voice, and it sounded like he was threatening Rasul's life or something to that affect. He wasn't quite sure he understood it the first time, so he listened to it again, and that made it even more puzzling.

"What rolls on four wheels with no motor?" the riddle plagued him before finally registering. "What rolls on four wheels with no motor?" The question echoed in Rasul's mind, and then it hit him.

"Oh shit, Dog!" he panicked.

Rasul dialed Dog's number back to back to back, and there was no answer. "Damn!" He started to worry. "Where da fuck are you at Dog?" he said, dialing the number again, and still no answer.

He gave up and called Pretty E. "Pretty E, have you talked to Dog?" he asked him.

"Nah, why? Whass'up?" Pretty E asked, sensing the urgency in his voice.

"Cause I just received a crazy message from the boah Mike Cottman," Rasul said.

"What he say?" Pretty E asked.

"What has four wheels and no motor?"

"Dog," Pretty E replied immediately. "I told you to stop fuckin' wit' dat boy's wife. Dat young boy is stupid, straight up gun-ho."

"Man, fuck dat nigga! He ain't crazy," Rasul said, before adding, "I'm gun-ho too!"

"I know dat's right," Pretty E said, and him and Rasul decided to meet at Dog's because he wasn't answering.

When they got to Dog's house, Rasul saw just how sick and deranged Mike really was. Only a sick man could do what was done to Dog, and Mike was the sickest. Rasul and Pretty E tears hadn't stop falling yet.

■■■■■■

Homicides had been becoming just as regular as simple misdemeanors in the new millennium, and most were unsolved. Although there was more cases solved then opened, there was one that still bothered Detective Cohn every single day. That was the murder of his partner, Detective Armstrong. Now there was this one, and from the looks of it, it would go unsolved too. There was no motive, no weapon, no witness, nothing. So, as Detective Cohen combed the crime scene frustrated, and a natural hate for these type of crimes overcame him, because he indeed was an officer of the law. It went against everything he fought so hard to prevent, solve and convict the guilty. But as he looked at this victim, who had died with his eyes open, and in obvious fear, he almost felt good. Felt good because he knew that somehow, someway, Dog was one of the ones responsible for his partner's death. Yet, he still had a job to do…solving a crime.

## Chapter Fourteen

The house on Vandever Avenue had been closed for nearly three years. The bust that took place there that day on Dog and Pretty E had Rasul contemplating selling the joint, but he hadn't come to a conclusion. So it just sat vacant. But now, since Pretty E had received the order from Rasul to put Jaquaan on, it was back open for business.

Jaquaan, Boog and O.D.B. had only opened the house about four days ago, and already the word was out. Crack cooked down to the oils was the only thing coming from out of this house, and the spot was jumping like never before. Jaquaan was the new top dog, and he quickly earned the name "Lil' Rasul" by the streets.

"Right here, girl. Park right here," Slim told Chyna Doll, when they pulled up to the house.

"Girl, I hope this shit ain't garbage," Chyna Doll said. "Cause I'll be damn if I'm tryin' to waste my damn money."

"Girl, this is straight drop and pop. Girl, these ma'fuckas got '88' coke."

"Bitch, I wasn't getting high in the 80s. Now here, go get a $30 cent piece," Chyna Doll said.

"Bitch, you might as well spend the fifty and get a sixteenth," Slim said.

"Alright, here. But, bitch, this is it. I ain't going to be smokin' coke all night. I'm going home early on you bitches."

"And you say that to say what?" Slim asked.

"To say, bitch, I ain't going to be getting high wit' you bitches all night into the next morning…birds up chirping and shit."

"Bitch, you crazy," Slim said, and started laughing. "Now come on, bitch, let's go get this and get up outta here."

Slim led the way, because it had been eons since Chyna Doll had been out, and walking with Slim she looked dead out of place. Her over a year clean and sober had her looking like she never touched a drug in her life. So, when they stepped into the house on Vandever Avenue, all eyes were on her.

"Damn, baby girl! You fine as hell! I know you don't get high," O.D.B. said.

"I know…and what is you doin' wit' Slim" Boog asked.

"What'chu mean what she doin' wit' me?" This is my mu'fuckin' girl. O.D.B. you know her. Boy, that's Chyna Doll."

"Get da fuck out of here!" O.D.B. snapped. "Damn, Chyna! Girl, you look good as hell. I fuck da shit out of you now," Boog assured her.

"Yeah, you will, if you got $200.00," Chyna Doll said.

"$200.00 my ass! I'll give your ass some of this hard," O.D.B. replied, causing Jaquaan and Boog to laugh.

"I don't fuck for drugs," Chyna Doll insisted.

"I catch dat ass late night you will."

"Whatever."

"Whass'up? What'chu need, Slim?" Jaquaan asked.

"I need a sixteenth," Slim said.

"Girl, you know we don't do sixteenths. It's straight quarters, halves and wholes. Them corner boys got dat shit," Jaquaan said.

"Com on, Lil' Rasul. You know I'm good people. Straighten me out," Slim said.

"Alright, I got you," he said.

"And you need to start comin' out to the motels wit' us. Nigga, it's big money out there. All them truck drivers and prostitutes and shit, you'll make a mint."

"You know I don't fuck around out them motels like dat. Them ma'fuckas is hot."

"Look, just give me your number anyway, just in case. Feel me?"

"Aright," Jaquaan said, passing her the sixteenth and his number.

Chyna Doll could barely wait to take another swerve, so as soon as they reached the car, she was pulling out her stem, the one Slim gave her.

"Damn, bitch, can we pull off first?" Slim said.

"Bitch, I need a pop now. I'm having a crack attack," Chyna Doll said.

"I see," Slim said, and broke a piece of the rock to put in her stem.

Chyna Doll flicked her bic and touched the end of her stem with the lighter, pulling the smoke into her lungs. Instantly, her ears began to ring, and her body pulsated everywhere, from the thumping of her heart. She was high as a kite, a feeling she hadn't had in a long time.

"You alright?" Slim asked, watching as Chyna Doll looked around suspiciously, and repeatedly checked her pockets over and over again.

"Yeah, I'm alright," Chyna Doll answered.

"Well, pull off then, bitch. Let's get outta here."

"Where we goin'?" Chyna Doll asked.

"Back to the motel and pick them bitches up," Slim said.

"Then what?"

"Then, we do what we do."

"And that is?"

"Hit the Avenue and the truck stops," Slim said.

"Which truck stop?"

"Either the one in New Jersey, the Pilot, or the Flying J."

"Bitch, we ain't going to do that all night," Chyna Doll said.

"I don't plan on it. I'm just tryin' to make a quick couple hundred on a couple dates," Slim said.

"I can go for that."

"Well, come on, let's go." And they were out of there.

■■■■■■

Chyna Doll and Slim were supposed to be going back to the Motel to pick up Flame, Blondie and Nikki up so they could hit the truck stops to make money. But after sitting down and smoking the rest of the sixteenth, they were stuck and not wanting to do anything else but smoke more crack. That's why Chyna Doll constantly hit the ATM machine until she exceeded the five hundred dollar limit.

"Damn," she cursed under her breath, as she crumpled up the receipt that spit from out of the machine. There was still plenty of money in both her accounts, checking and savings, that's why she was so upset when she got back to the car.

"Girl, that's fucked up. I don't understand that shit. How the bank goin' to tell you how much money of yours you can spend? Bitch, that's my money, I should be able to pull out as much as I want if I got it, you know?" Chyna Doll complained.

"So, what we goin' to do now?" Slim asked.

"Bitch, we goin' to do what we do."

■■■■■■

In New Jersey at the Flying J, Chyna Doll couldn't

believe that she was actually back out here. Just earlier today, she was dealing with professionals, now she was out here dealing with truckers.

At the parlor she was guaranteed at least $150.00 minimum, for anything she did. Now she was lucky to get $50.00 for a blow job. Actually, she wasn't expecting anything less. So now, as she stepped down out of her second date's tractor-trailer, she securely tucked her money away in her bra, then her phone rang.

Again, it was one of the three...Snow White, Tammy or Monique. They had been calling all day. She knew after she didn't answer the phone the first couple of times, they'd be worried. She could hear them now, "I hope she ain't relapsing." But it was too late for that. She was in full blown relapse mode. She just hoped she could end this episode tonight, and get back on track.

After the third date, Chyna Doll became frustrated. She had barely over a hundred dollars.

"Fuck this shit," she told herself. "The next mu'fucka is getting robbed." She began her stroll. She didn't even make it across the street, and a truck's lights were already flashing her to accompany them in their rig. "Got'em," Chyna said, and strutted across the parking lot.

"Hey cutie," she said, once inside the truck. "Whass'up? You want some company?"

"Yeah."

"What kind of company do you want?" she asked.

"I don't know," the truck said shyly.

"Awww, baby, it's alright. You don't have to be shy, just say it. You want some pussy, or do you want a blow job?"

"How much will it cost?" the trucker asked.

"Well, I do blow jobs for $50.00, and I fuck for $100.00."

"I don't have a hundred, so I'll take a blow job," he said.

"Well, you have to pay me up front."

"Okay. I have no problem with that," the trucker said, and peeled a fifty from his wallet.

Chyna Doll's eyes lit up. The story the man said about having no money was a bold face lie.

"This mu'fucka is loaded," Chyna Doll said to herself, heart pounding with anxiety for what she was about to do.

She hadn't pulled this stunt in a while, so she hoped she still had it. She followed the man into the cab of the truck. She fiddled with his belt to get his pants down around his ankles, then went to work. As she moved, she realized she hadn't lost a beat. She started by grabbing his dick, then putting the rubber in her mouth. With no hands, she placed it on his erect dick and moved her head up and down, while looking into the man's eyes. Mesmerized, the man let his head fall back, and Chyna Doll knew it was now or never.

Using her free hand, she slid it into the man's back pocket, and slid her fingers into his wallet. She felt the money that was neatly lined in the wallet's slot, and like clock work, she peeled the bills.

"Wa-la," she said, and placed the money in her back pocket, just as the man's cum filled the condom.

"There you go," Chyna Doll said. "Enjoy?" she asked.

"Loved it," he said.

"Good. Here, give me a call," she said, and handed him a bogus number.

Realizing the girl he was with was a prostitute, he felt for his wallet in his back pocket. When he was sure it was there, he let her out of his truck. What he didn't know was when he went to pay for something, there wouldn't be any money. Chyna Doll was gone, fifteen hundred dollars richer than when she came.

■■■■■■

Relax Sinsations was open, up and running on time, but still there was no Chyna Doll. Tammy, Snow White and Monique were beyond the point of being mad, they were now beginning to worry about her safety. They came to the conclusion, and made their minds up that Chyna Doll had indeed relapsed. They were just wondering now how bad the lapse was. Was it just a one day thing, or was it the start of a binge.

"After my next appointment, I'm going to look for her," Monique said.

"We all might as well go," Snow White suggested.

"Yeah, that's a good idea. We'll just close up early, that's all," Tammy said.

"That's whass'up," Monique said, then cut her eye at Tammy.

She had been doing that a lot lately, and Tammy was beginning to take notice. Notice of everything Monique was doing, like getting grumpy when Pretty E came around, and saying little sarcastic shit under her breath. Tammy was fighting with everything she had in her not to give into Monique's advances, but she knew she wouldn't be able to do it much longer.

Fact was that she had fallen in love with Monique from the first they made love, and now she was beginning to miss her. She was reminded of it every time she made love to Pretty E. He just wasn't Monique, and she was beginning to fall out of love with him.

*Damn, not only am I gay, I'm in love with a white girl, especially after the way I acted about Lucy*, she thought. *Oh well,* she managed to think, and smiled at Monique's eye cut. Monique smiled back then blew her a kiss.

Tammy, Snow White and Monique checked every motel on the Avenue, Route 13 and Route 40, but they didn't see Chyna Doll at any of them. They repeated the same thing over and over for the next two hours, before finally giving up and deciding to call it a night. *Fuck it!* they all thought.

Right now, at this particular time, Chyna didn't want to be found.

## Chapter Fifteen

Rasul and Pretty E arrived at Dog's house, only to find it flooded with police, and surrounded with yellow tape. The message Mike left on the phone wasn't a fluke after all, he was dead serious. Rasul just hoped now that Dog was still alive. He and Pretty E tried to cross the police barriers, but was stopped by a detective. His name was Detective Cohen, and they were all too familiar with the middle aged white man, whose sole purpose seemed to be to fuck with them. It had been that way for years, ever since the death of his partner, Detective Armstrong.

"Sorry, gentlemen, but you can't come beyond this point," Detective Cohen said, stopping them in their tracks.

"Why?" Rasul asked.

"Because there has been a serious crime committed here tonight," Detective Cohen answered. "We're still trying to make sense of it all."

Truth was, they'd never be able to make sense of it all. There was nothing left behind. Not a motive, not a suspect, not a weapon, nothing. That just burned Detective Cohen up. This was the one thing he hated most about his job, not being able to make an arrest. Shit, he thought, just like the Jabor murder on Clayton Street, at the base house, his first ever case.

Just remembering that case alone had brought back some fond memories of his partner and mentor, Detective Armstrong. And despite all of the things that came out after his death, like the gambling debts, and his crookedness, nothing could change the way Detective Cohen felt about him.

"What kind of crime happened here tonight?" Rasul asked the Detective, and he leaped at the opportunity.

Even though he knew what he was about to do was wrong, he did it anyway. He couldn't wait to see the hurt and pain on their faces when he dropped the bomb. The same hurt and pain he had when they told him of Detective Armstrong's death.

"Your boy and partner, Mr. Mike Lolley a/k/a Dog was murdered tonight," he said with a grin, and watched as they fell a part. "How does it feel, guys? Probably like it felt when you murdered my partner. Pay back's a bitch, huh! Ha! Ha!," he laughed, and Rasul was on his ass.

The first blow caught the burly detective clean on the chin, causing him to stumble backwards. Before he realized what actually happened, Rasul was throwing another one. This one floored him, sending him straight on his wallet. The other officers on the scene were so busy combing the area for clues, that they hadn't realized what was happening until Detective Cohen was being pounded on by Rasul. Even then they didn't break their necks to get over there to save him.

Detective Cohen had earned a reputation as being a wise guy, or a smart ass. The precinct called him the "Captains Pet", so he wasn't everybody's favorite. So, watching the little melee take place was more than appeasing to his fellow officers. When they finally broke up the tussle, Detective Cohen was a black eyed, bloodied mouth wise ass who still had a smart mouth.

"That still won't bring Dog back, you stupid fuck!" Detective shouted.

"Yeah, now Dog can meet his victim face to face, pussy! I wish now I'da been the one to pull da trigger!" Rasul shot back, finally clearing the question that went unanswered in Detective Cohen's head. Dog was the one who took his partner's life that night, and the words were like daggers through Detective Cohen's heart.

■■■■■■

Mike Cottman, in his always calm manner, was nearly a Hannibal Lector type of character. Even now, as he drove home from just murdering another one of his victims, his heart rate and pulse still beat normally. There wasn't an emotion inside of him for anything or anybody in this world, except his family, children, his wife, Ann, and Tommy Good. So now, as he parked the Hurst and got back into his normal Mercedes R-500, and not the black Celebrity, he felt good knowing that that has been ass nigga, Rasul, was probably balling out tears somewhere like a bitch.

Fuck him, Mike thought, as he reached his house. He placed the key in the door and there she stood, dressed in a Delta Airlines flight attendant's outfit. He smiled.

"I thought I'd let you relive our flight to Africa, the way you and Tommy were staring at that stewardess. So why do you say? Will you be flying Delta today?" Ann asked her husband.

"Yes, I will, first class," Mike answered, and swooped her off her feet.

The lovemaking they encountered that evening was as good to each other as the first time they ever made love to one another. And yes indeed it felt to the both of them as if they were flying 30,000 feet in the sky. When they were finished, they both heard the words, thank you for flying Delta, and fell asleep in each other's arms.

■■■■■■

Once the police department, news vans, and spectators that formed a circus outside of Dog's house cleared out for the evening, Kim and her children sat in the living room wondering why. Why was her husband and their father taken away from them like that? Rasul and Pretty E sat before them, trying to console them, but their guilt of knowing why, how and who was responsible for his death had ate at them more than they realized it would.

To them, Mike Cottman, Tommy Good, or one of them had to be dealt with, and dealt with sooner rather than later. The question to them now, was how. They knew in their heart of hearts that they'd be the ones to handle the killing, because that would be the only way to get the full gratification of avenging their brother's, Dog, death. They just had been out of the streets for so long now, they wondered if a war or beef was what they needed at this point in their lives. The answer came back just as fast as the question appeared. Fucking right beef was the only thing left to do. Mike Cottman or Tommy Good was about to feel the raft of some true O.G. gangster ass niggaz. One who had already took out an entire Mafia family. Rasul and Pretty E were thinkers, and their minds were in overdrive.

# Chapter Sixteen

Chyna Doll had tapped her Mac card for the umpteenth time this week. And in shame, a tear fell from her eye and stained her cheek with the black eyeliner she wore. A one day escapade to find some of her old friends to come work at the Relax Sinsations, had turned into a week long binge.

She hadn't eaten a good meal since her and Flame ate those meatball subs from Wawa. Her meals now consisted of quarter juices and Little Debbie Snacks, sometimes some potato chips or some'em. Right now she could barely keep her eyes open. Almost in a state of delirium, she got back in her BMW, that now looked like a hurricane had spun through it with her girls, Flame, Blondie and Slim.

"Where to now?" Chyna Doll asked.

"We need to be going to a car wash," Slim answered, looking around at all the trash, broken stem glasses and Chore Boy shavings that had accumulated over the week.

"Yeah, we can do that, but first go out to the Hollywood Hotel to see my baby, First. I know he doin' some'um," Blondie suggested.

■■■■■■

The Hollywood Hotel on Route 13 was notorious for prostitution. The little shabby horseshoe shaped motel on Route 13 right before the 13-40 split was, as usual, packed with cars today, and the red No Vacancy sign flicked off and on.

Chyna Doll pulled the BMW up in front of Room 119 and parked, and just as they were exiting the car, they saw another one of their girls, Ms. L.L., coming from out of the room.

"Whass'up, bitch?" Chyna Doll asked her girl of years.

"Ain't shit, and As-Salaam-Alaikum," L.L., the tall blonde bombshell of a white girl said.

"Is my baby in there?" Blondie asked, referring to the boah First.

"Yeah, he in there," L.L. replied.

"Good," Blondie said.

Barely even up to the door, a champagne color Honda Civic, with a black dude and Spanish dude pulled up. Feeling bad that she had been gone all night long, and not having any money for First, she decided to date the two in the car.

"Y'all go ahead in the room. Tell my baby I'll be right back," Blondie said, and jumped in the back seat. "So whass'up? What'chall want to do? Do y'all want some pussy or some head?"

"We want some pussy," they both answered immediately.

"Alright. Now y'all know that's a hundred a piece, and I need to be paid first," she told them, and they passed her two crisp one hundred dollar bills, before pulling off.

With the money secured away in her bra, Blondie was looking for an out. "Fuck dating," she told herself. "I already got the money now." So, as soon as the car stopped at its first red light, Blondie was jumping out and running down the shoulder back toward the Hollywood.

"Bitch!" the Spanish boy yelled. "You better give me my money!" he shouted, and started to get out, but decided against it.

That would bring too much attention to him if he chased her down the highway shoulder. He was sure a passerby would dial 911 and he'd be going down. So, instead, they made the u-turn and headed back to the Hollywood, where they first picked her up.

Blondie knocked on Room 119 door harder than usual. "Open the door, hurry up!" she shouted.

First opened the door to find his baby standing before him. His first instinct was to smack the shit out of her for not coming home last night, but he decided against it because here she stood now. Had he knew she was with baldhead Johns all night smoking coke he woulda.

"Why da fuck is you knocking like that?" First snapped.

"Because First, I mean Daddy," she said, buttering him up, "I just got these two dudes for two hundred," she said proudly.

"Well, where's my money?" he asked.

"Right here," she said, and retrieved the two hundred dollar bills from her bra. "Don't answer the door. Okay, Daddy? Cause I think they might be coming here, okay."

"Fuck'em," First said, and locked the door behind her.

"Girl, why would you draw on the room like that?" Slim asked Blondie.

"Fuck'em! We just ain't goin' to open the door," she replied, and it seemed as if the door was coming down.

"Boom! Boom! Boom!" sounded the door when the brother knocked.

"Who da fuck is it? And why da fuck is you beatin' on my door like dat?" First asked.

"It's Killer and Bear," the brother, Bear, answered. "Where dat white bitch at?"

"What white bitch, nigga!" First snapped, opening the door, then stepped out into the dark because the light was off in the hallway. "Don't be banging on this door for no white bitch, nigga!" First said, and stepped between the two of them on his way outside. Armed with a cane and smoking a cigarette, he walked down to Pockets and L.L.'s room.

"Man, some'em gotta give. Either that nigga or dat bitch goin' to do some'um," Killer said, and they jumped in the car.

Riding out of the motel parking lot, they wanted to jump out on First, but decided against it.

So Killer just rolled down the window and said to First, "We'll be back."

Little did they know the name First was short for First Degree, but they'd soon find out.

■■■■■■

First hadn't even finished his cigarette before the Honda Civic pulled back up. He looked to the two dudes he had come to know as Killer and Bear, and smirked at them as if to say, "Y'all don't really want it", but they stopped and out jumped Bear. First just continued to grin. Had Bear known that, not only was First carrying a cane, but had an eight-inch dagger belted to his arm, he might have thought twice, but he didn't.

Bear charged at First, only to be picked apart by him. He didn't know his hand skills were that up to par. So after being hit with a barrage of punches, and being showed up in front of his boy, killer, he ran across the intersection, away from the motel.

Killer, the Spanish boah, couldn't believe that his boy, Bear, had run, so he jumped out to handle First. Using his height advantage, he jabbed away at First, catching him cleaning with some solid shots, only making First angrier, because he was being showed up in front of his bottom ho Blondie. That's when First flashed the dagger with the swiftness of a born killer.

First swung the dagger. Swoosh, it sounded as it cut the air. Swoosh, it sounded again, missing Killer by inches. Then it happened...Killer threw a wild hook, leaving himself wide open, and First seized the opportunity. Swoosh, he swung again, only this time the dagger caught Killer cleanly on the side of his head, right above the temple. In shock, not knowing what just happened, just shocked he had been hit, Killer began swinging wildly. And in less than a minute, he was falling down from a loss of blood. First was on him, he stomped Killer's head with bad intention, and stepped off when he was sure Killer was knocked all the way out.

Once he was sure, he stepped off, not knowing he was leaving a bloody trail of boot prints back to his room.

"Oh my God, baby! Are you a'ight? Here, come'ere," Blondie said, and her and the rest of the girls, including L.L. cleaned him up.

Blondie, Chyna Doll and Slim began to bleach and clean everything in sight, while Flame and L.L. got rid of the dagger, the boots, and the bloody blanket.

When they were sure everything was good, they looked outside. Killer was still lying in the same spot, and this was nearly an hour later. So, out of sympathy, First flagged down a state trooper, who had already had a person pulled over on a traffic stop. By First having a heart, and trying to get the boy some help, helped him out later in court.

The state charged First with a negligence homicide, and he received three years. He'll be home in eighteen months.

But right now, there laid a body in the middle of the Hollywood Motel's parking lot, and it was too much for the girls to stomach. First, sensing the girls' worriedness kind of huddled them all together to comfort them, but it barely worked.

"Come on y'all, let's go in the room," he said, as the paramedics were zipping Killer up in the body bag.

That was what had done it for Chyna Doll. The binge was over. Seeing someone just get killed was the straw that broke the camel's back, and not just for her either. Flame, L.L., Slim and Blondie all wanted out of the life they were living. So when Chyna Doll called Tammy, Snow White and Monique at Relax Sinsations, she was ready to be picked up…her and the other four to work the empty booths, but not until they all left the Detox Center on Kirkwood Highway that Tammy, Snow White and Monique dropped them off at. And like always, Nurse Pat and Nurse Crystal were there to check them in.

## Chapter Seventeen

Davita couldn't believe she had mustered up enough courage to tell Tommy about Rasul, but she had. She never suspected that in doing so, that Tommy would lay a hand on her, but he had. What he didn't know that in doing so, he would lose his wife forever. Davita's heart now had dark spots like a soccer ball on it for him, and there was no winning her over.

So, as she drove recklessly towards her safe haven, Rasul's house, with tears still falling from her eyes, the only thing she could think of was you reap what you sow. She couldn't wait to tell Rasul about the events that happened just moments ago. What she didn't know was that, at this very moment, the biggest war in the state's history was about to take place, and she was the Queen piece like in one big chess game that had been capture by the O.G. Rasul would use this Queen for an across the board checkmate on this nigga, Tommy Good or Mike Cottman.

Rasul had just gotten in the house and barely had time to kick off his shoes and get settled in, before he noticed the headlights shine through the kitchen window from the driveway. A visitor right now was the last thing he wanted, especially after watching Dog being zipped up and hauled off in the coroner's van. However, when he noticed it was Davita, he had a change of heart. Not only did he want to see her because he had missed her company all day, he wanted to see her to have a shoulder to lean on and someone to cry to about Dog's death. Not to mention gain some leverage on this dude, Mike Cottman, check.

"Hey baby," Rasul said, greeting Davita at the door.

By her not even being able to knock had put a smile on her face, because that must have meant that Rasul was expecting her.

Trying her best to conceal what had happened to her, she smiled even harder, then said, "Well, hello to you too, baby." She stepped into his outstretched arms. The hug they shared had a little more feeling than their usual embraces, and they both sensed it. The thing now was who'd be the one to reveal their mishap.

"Whass'up? Why you ain't call me all day?" Rasul asked. "I just woke up to you gone from my bedside," he spoke, not revealing what happened.

Then Davita broke the ice. "I couldn't. I got in this huge fight with Tommy about staying out all night. He said some'um slick, I said some'um slick. Then I told him about us," she said.

"What he say?" Rasul asked.

"He hit me, that's what he did," Davita said, and the tears began to fall. "I swear to God on my brother's grave, I wish I never met that bastard! I hate him, Rasul. I swear I do," she cried, burying her face into his chest as he squeezed her tightly.

"Don't' worry about it, baby, I got dat nigga. I got him and that nigga, Mike," Rasul assured her.

"Why would you say that? What are you going to do about it? And why would you want to do some'um about it? I mean, he ain't done nuffin' to you," Davita said.

"The fuck he didn't! He put his hands on my baby, plus that nigga, Mike," he said.

"Uh-huh," she said.

"The one that followed us that day."

"Uh-huh, Tommy's boy."

"Yeah, dat nigga killed my boy tonight. Listen to this," Rasul said, and let her hear the saved message.

After hearing the voice, there was no denying it was Mike. She looked at Rasul and felt as though it was her fault Dog was gone.

"Baby, I'm sorry," she said.

"Don't be, it wasn't your fault."

"But, but…" she started to say, before Rasul cut her off.

"But nuffin' at all. I'ma handle these niggaz. I just may need a little help," Rasul said.

"Whatever it is I can do, I will," the Queen spoke.

Check, Rasul thought. Check.

■■■■■■

Dog's murder was almost unbelievable to the City of Wilmington. Unbelievable to them, because how could such an icon in the 'hood be taken off the map, especially after doing all the things he did. The most memorable to the streets was the M.O.B. slaying that left him paralyzed. Now cars lined the streets for blocks to say farewell to Dog's last showing at the Ebenezer Baptist Church.

The funeral that was about to take place was something out of a movie. It was as if Big Poppa was having another viewing and service today. But he wasn't, this was Dog's day and he was to Delaware what Big Poppa was to New York, and PAC was to California.

Dog's funeral was so big that they had a two day viewing. Today though was the day he would be laid to rest, and even more was in attendance. The future Mayor Mr. Robert Bovell was in attendance, a true pillar in the community. Mayor Sills was there. The Journal and Philadelphia Inquirer was in attendance, and every 'hood superstar on the east coast was there. Even Baltimore's own Carmello Anthony came to show his respect to the fallen 'hood legend.

Dog sat laying at the front of the church, right beneath the pulpit in a casket similar to the one Hit-Man was buried in years ago. Twenty-four carats to be exact made up the outer layer of the coffin, while jet black satin lined the inside. Dog, himself, was dressed in linen by Armani, rocked Ostrich and Crocodile shoes, was draped in every diamond he'd ever bought, and wore a 2007 frame by Dolce and Gabbana. He looked at peace.

The organ pipes blew as the church began to fill up, and before you knew it, people were lining the walls because the church benches had been long filled.

"May everyone rise as the family of the departed make their way into the Lord's house. And now that I walk through the shadows of death, I shall fear no evil," the preacher shouted aloud, as if to wart off any evil in the building.

Once the family viewed their loved one, they were seated. Rasul, Tammy, Pretty E, Davita, Kim, Big Trina, Jaquaan, Dog's children, brother and sister, along with other family members, all filled the first three rows of the church on both sides of the aisle. The preacher stood up behind the pulpit, looked out into the sea of spectators, and couldn't believe his eyes...the funeral was enormous. He hadn't seen a funeral this big in all the days of his life. The church had to actually hook up loud speakers outside for those who weren't able to get into the church. So seeing this, the preacher spoke into the microphone for the first time.

"Before we begin the celebration and farewell party to brother Michael 'Dog' Collie, I would like to call a final viewing and give us all a last chance to say goodbye," he shouted. "To our friend, our family member, our brother," and a line formed from around the church to outside the church. One by one, they passed Dog's casket for the last time. Some took pictures to remember the icon, some took mental pictures, while others tossed memorabilia of themselves into the coffin with him. There were pictures of girls, rolls and rolls of money, jewelry, pieces of clothing, anything you could name. They all wanted Dog to take a piece of them to Heaven with him.

Today was just a fucked up day. And the questions who and why would someone do this, were quickly answered in the streets, and nearly confirmed when they saw Davita sitting next to Rasul. Apparently Rasul and Davita had become a couple, so Tommy wanted revenge. He sent Mike, rumor has it, to kill Dog in cold blood. The church went silent.

■■■■■■

The whispers began outside the church the moment they pulled up. People couldn't believe the nerve of these two, as the Black Celebrity, known as the Hurst, pulled up to the side of the building and parked by a fire exit door. Tommy Good and Mike Cottman were as dapper as anyone who ever graced the pages of any G.Q. magazine. In matching Salvator Farragomma suits, they strutted up to the church and walked through the front doors. Their entrance nearly sucked the breath out of the church.

*The nerve of these niggaz!* Rasul and Pretty E thought at the same time. However, they chose not to react and disrespect their boy's going away party. Tommy and Mike would de dealt with though. With sarcastic looks on their faces and tiny grins on their lips, only fueled the fire that had became an inferno inside of Rasul and Pretty E. But what happened next would be the most disrespectful thing anyone has ever bore witness to, as Tommy and Mike reached the casket.

Tommy and Mike stood before the casket, looking in on another piece of Mike's work. It was almost formality like for anyone to be knocked off that cross Tommy Good, and Dog was no different. No one was untouchable or out of reach of Mike Cottman. So when they were tired of looking in on what Mike had become accustomed to calling "has beens", it happened.

Mike drew a snot-laced hawker from the depth of his throat and spit it right between the eyes of the dead man. Before the spit could even slide down Dog's face and find its resting spot in his ear lobe, Mike was snatching his twin .45 caliber pistols from the small of his back. No one in the church was prepared for an act like that. So, as Mike spun around on his heels and unloaded--his targets, Rasul and Pretty E.

Boom! Boom! Boom! Boom! Boom! The first five shots sounded from Mike's gun. The first bullet ripped through the chamber, glazing Rasul on the shoulder and knocking a piece of wood clean off the church bench. The others found their resting places in the church walls as people dove over benches, crawled on the floor, and nearly stampeded one another trying to escape the bullets with no names on them.

*Boom! Boom! Boom!* The onslaught continued by Mike, as Tommy's laugh echoed through the preacher's microphone on the pulpit. Tommy looked at Davita, the only one still seated in the church, and blew a kiss as he and Mike escaped through the fire exit door, where the Hurst waited for them.

When the smoke cleared, the church was a mess. Bullet holes pierced the walls and benches. Bibles were flung all over the place, and never ending screams still filled the air. What just happened was the beginning of the end for Tommy Good and Mike Cottman… or was it?

## Chapter Eighteen

Two weeks had passed, and the events that took place at Dog's funeral were still the talk of the town. Rasul and Pretty E had been so preoccupied with revenge on Tommy and Mike, that they were neglecting their loved ones, and Tammy was beginning to take notice of her own wants and needs that were being denied.

"Why da fuck are you ignoring me?" she asked Pretty E. "I mean, I know it's bad timing and everything, but damn, baby, what about me? I ain't been out of jail six months yet, and I feel like you're getting tired of me."

"How can you be so damn inconsiderate, Tammy? Huh? Why da fuck does it always have to be about you?" Pretty E asked.

"What? I know you ain't just say that? Are you serious?"

"As a heart attack," he said.

"Oh, okay. I see…I see I have to have my needs catered to some other way then, huh? You know what? Fuck you, Eric!"

"My boy was just murdered, Tammy!" Pretty E yelled.

"And so was Lucy and Frankie and Hit-Man and Tameeka, nigga! You should be used to it by now," she said, and slammed the door behind her.

Pretty E couldn't believe or begin to understand why Tammy was tripping so much lately. Had he known she was crying out to him for attention, because she herself was becoming confused, he would have paid it more mind. Tammy was lost in a love triangle between Pretty E and Monique, and Monique was winning the tug-of-war battle.

By the time Tammy reached Relax Sinsations, she had basically regained her composure. Pulling down the sun visor, she looked in the mirror and straightened herself out. There was no way she wanted to let Monique know she was winning, because Tammy still told herself that she wasn't gay.

"Hey everybody," Tammy greeted everyone as she entered the parlor.

"Hey sister," Snow White spoke. "Guess what?"

"What?" Tammy asked.

"I just talked to Chyna Doll, and her, Blondie, L.L., Flame and Slim will be home from the thirty-day program next week. So, for the first time since we been open, we'll be running at full capacity."

"Oh, that's whass'up," Tammy said, as Monique walked out with another satisfied customer. "Hey Mo," Tammy spoke, but Monique didn't respond, she just rolled her eyes, and kept on keeping on. What's her problem, Tammy thought.

Monique was almost tempted to speak to Tammy, but decided not to. She was tired of being the rebound bitch. She was too emotionally involved with Tammy to allow the constant running back and forth between herself and Pretty E. It was time for a choice.

"Mo, why are you acting shady?" Tammy asked, following Monique to the back booth that she ran.

"Why do you care? You're not gay, remember?" she said, with a laugh. "You're strictly dickly, huh? Or strictly clitly and strap on?"

"Why are you being so mean?" Tammy asked.

"I'm not, I'm just learning to love me just a little bit more, that's all," Monique replied.

"Well, you know I love you, don't you?"

"Do you, or did that no good ass nigga of yours just let you know how unimportant to him you are?" There was silence. "Just like I thought," Monique said, turning to walk out of the booth.

"Mo wait! Don't walk away from me, I need you," Tammy said, and grabbed her from behind.

Slowly Tammy grind her hips onto Monique's ass, sending blood to each one of her nerve endings. Then Monique turned around. Their kiss was like the first one they shared in jail, only this time it felt better. Love was between their kiss, and they both could feel it.

■■■■■■

Frankie "Lil' Frank" Maraachi the third, was an eighteen year old hot-headed Italian, whose grandfather happened to be Frankie Maraachi, the boss of all bosses of the Capelli family. With gorgeous looks like his late great grandfather, Lil' Frank had a way with women, and his temper reminded people of his great-great uncle, Albert Anestasia…The Mad Hatter.

With qualities like that, Lil' Frank quickly put together a team of young Italians, whose drug selling, smash and grab jewelry heists, and bullying local businesses, had made them something to be reckoned with.

Now, as the meeting was about to take place at the newly renovated Lil' Italy bar and lounge, Lil' Frank was pulling up in his black on black drop top Maserati. Jumping out of his car, that he illegally parked in the middle of the street with the hazards light on, Lil' Frank looked more like a rap star than a mobster. His Rocawear jeans sagged slightly off his ass, revealing his Joe Boxer briefs and spiked Roc belt. His white wife beater T-shirt matched his low top white on white shell top Adidas, and revealed his olive skin complexion and rock solid frame. Both his arms, from the hands clean up around his shoulders and neck and down his back, were completely covered with tattoos. Lil' Frank shut the car door behind him and bobbed into Lil' Italy to start the meeting.

"Whass'up, y'all?" Lil' Frank began. "As we all know, there's a big war going on across town between the Moolies… Rasul and Tommy Good. And you know we're rooting for Tommy Good, because those mutha-fuckas, Rasul, Pretty E and Dog were responsible, I still think to this day, for the murder of my great grandfather. The moolie does, however, have a son. His name is Jaquaan or Lil' Rasul as they call him in the streets. He runs with these two niggaz named Boog and O.D.B.. That's our rival enemies. We're going to take them out the same way his father took out my grandfather. Revenge is a must! It's the sweetest joy, next to getting pussy," Lil' Frank said, and walked out the door. "We'll talk about it more later. For now, let's root for Tommy.

■■■■■■

"Yo, I still can't believe dat shit! Them niggaz really is gangsta!" Boog spoke at the house on Vandever Avenue about Tommy Good and Mike Cottman.

"It ain't really Tommy, it's da nigga Mike," O.D.B. added. "Yo, dat nigga cold blooded spit in a dead man's face. How real is dat? Then the nigga had a nerve to dump on the whole church. Nigga, dat's gangsta!"

"Fuck dem niggaz!" Jaquaan spoke. "My pop and Pretty E goin' to handle dat shit! Word on my mom's," he finished, tired of hearing his boys glorify dem niggaz, Tommy and Mike.

"Oh, fo'sho. We know Rasul and Pretty E goin' to handle dat. We just sayin' dat was some gangsta ass shit," O.D.B. replied.

"Nigga, y'all ain't seen gangsta," Jaquaan replied, knowing his dad had some'em in store for their asses.

Thing was though, these three youngin's who were filling the shoes of Rasul, Dog and Pretty E never knew that on the other side of town in Lil' Italy they were being plotted on. What Lil' Frank didn't know was that these three niggaz, Jaquaan, Boog and

O.D.B. was just as heartless as the men whose shoes they were filling. But he'd soon find out.

## Chapter Nineteen

Bank-Shots, the pool hall, bar and lounge was located on the Hill Top section of the city on the Italian side of 4th Street. 4th Street was the dividing line that separated the Spanish, the Blacks, the Italians and the Whites. Eighth and Union Street was the location every Thursday night for a more than happening time out with every 'hood superstar and bad bitch in the city, and tonight was no different...the place was packed.

Being the center of attention every where he went, and having a reputation as the gangterest gangsta since Lil' Nikki Scarfo terrorized the streets of Philadelphia, Lil' Frank sat parked dead center of Bank-Shots parking lot. With his top down and rims still spinning, Lil' Frank nodded his head to The Petey Crack Files, Part III.

"Yo, dis my nigga! Petey Crack is dat nigga, nigga," Lil' Frank spoke to his boy Fat Sal.

"Fuckin' right," Fat Sal said. "Dat's all I fuck wit'...Petey Crack, Oschino and Meek Mills."

"Yo, yo!" Lil' Frank hollered across the lot. "Come'ere, baby girl!" he called out to the light skin girl he knew from school.

"Whass'up?" she asked the deep complexioned Italian boy she knew to be Frankie from school. But damn, how he has filled out, she thought to herself.

"Ain't your name Kia or some'um like dat?" Lil' Frank asked the girl, when she was standing next to his car.

"Yeah, Frankie, it's me." She laughed.

"Oooh shit! Girl, let me get out and give you a hug," he said, but she kept looking back over her shoulder. "What's wrong? What, your dude out here?" Lil' Frank asked.

"No, not yet," Kia said.

"Well, come give me a hug then with your sexy ass." The two of them embraced.

No sooner than they found comfort in each other's arms, the S.L. 500 Benz on dubs was rounding the corner. Since Lil' Frank's Maserati was parked dead center in the lot, that's the first thing they saw.

"Yo, ain't dat yo' bitch?" Jaquaan said to Boog, as they pulled up.

"Damn right dat's yo' bitch," O.D.B. said. "Boog, you need to smack da fire out dat bitch ass! Word you do!" O.D.B. instigated, as Jaquaan came to a halt right in front of the Maserati.

"Yo bitch! How da fuck you goin' to disrespect me like dat?" Boog snapped, as he jumped out the car. Kia stood stark still. She knew how Boog could get. "Get da fuck away from dat cracker's car," he said, and pushed her to the side to face the white boy.

"Cracker! Cracker! I'm damn near darker than your girl,

nigga! The girl that's about to be mine, you keep treatin' her like you do, nigga," Lil' Frank said, making Kia feel special.

"What?" Boog asked.

"You heard me!" Lil' Frank said, and swung on Boog, catching him flush on the jaw.

*This white boy got balls*, Boog thought, as they squared up in the parking lot. The two of them went at it for a good ten minutes. Blow for blow they went, until Jaquaan and O.D.B. couldn't stand no more. They leaped from the car to assist their boy, only to be greeted by Fat Sal and a whole slew of other Italians in Lil' Frank's M.O.B., The New Capelli's. They were clearly outnumbered, and knew it as they began to get their asses whipped.

"Yo, is dat Jaquaan and them?" S. Dot, cousin Shawn McNeil from 22nd and Carter asked.

"I think so," Munch said.

"Well, come on then, nigga. They from our 'hood," S. Dot said about Jaquaan, Boog and O.D.B., who were posted on Vandever Avenue, a block away from 22nd Street.

The boah's from Duece Duece couldn't have came any sooner for Jaquaan and them, as they about evened the scored and turned the beat down into a rumble. When the gun shots started going off, the crowd began to clear, and in the parking lot laid a Capelli Family member, Fat Sal, but he'd live.

"Aye yo! Yo Sammy! Put Fat Sal in your truck and get him out of here. Take him to Crozer Medical up Chester. We don't want these Delaware cops knowing nuffin'. Nuffin' at all," Lil' Frank said, then noticed Kia and two of her girlfriends still there in the parking lot.

"Y'all a'ight?" Lil' Frank asked, about to leave the scene.

'No, we need a ride home. My girl's car got the tires shot out," Kia answered.

"Whose?"

"Mine," Carmen, the Spanish girl said.

"Don't worry about it. I'll pay for it to get fixed, and all dat shit. Beings though I'm responsible and all," Lil' Frank said.

"Is your friend okay?" Kia asked about Fat Sal.

"He'll live. I can't say the same about the niggaz that did it though," and Kia, Carmen and Shontaé all got the message.

■■■■■■

This was the seventh straight day this week, actually from Monday to Monday, that they'd been together. He just couldn't get enough of this redhead he'd met the day he went to pick up his fianceé, Tammy, but she had already left with Snow White. But when he got there, Monique was locking up Relax Sinsations because she had the last client that day.

"Hey, whass'up? What, you closing up?" he asked.

Yeah, why? Would you like to make an appointment?"

"Monique asked.

"No, I'm actually here to pick up my fiancé, Tammy," Pretty E replied.

"Oh, so you're Pretty E? Now I can personally thank you for the money to get us up and started here at Relax Sinsations," Monique said.

"A thank you isn't needed. Just a small date off the record would do. You know I got a thing for white girls ever since my child's mother, Lucy."

"I think we can arrange that," Monique obliged, and they hadn't stopped fuckin' since.

Like now, as she screamed from the top of her lungs for him to stop as she came yet another time, only fueling Pretty E's animalistic instinct to fulfill her more.

"Damn, I love you, Daddy!" she screamed.

"And Daddy loves you back," he said, and hurriedly got dressed to go home.

"When are you going to tell her about us?" Monique asked.

"As soon as you give her an ultimatum," he shot back.

"Well, that will be tomorrow, I promise," Monique said, but tomorrow never came.

■■■■■■

Bolo, the sixty-five pound pit bull was the only thing Rasul had left of Hit-Man of his own to remember him by. The once perky and hyper pit bull pup that won him thousands of dollars, was now old and graying around the snout. He had become a house dog, and Lil' Tameeka loved playing with him. Now, as he limped around the yard aging daily, he found a spot under the shade tree in the front yard.

Lil' Frank saw the dog lay down near the fence, and knew it was now or never. With his car door still opened, he leaped from the car with a huge potato sack. In one swift leap, barely touching the fence, he was in Rasul's front yard, and tying Bolo up in the bag. Just like he came, he left and drove off to the garage where Fat Sal and Sammy were waiting.

As soon as they heard the car nearing, they were lifting the garage door. Immediately the chainsaw came to life, and off came Bolo's head. Still dripping with blood, Lil' Frank tossed it back into the sack and stuck a note to the side of it that read:

"This is what we do to moolies and muttz!

Capelli Family"

Once that was complete, Lil' Frank left again to complete the job. He dropped the head off at the house on Vandever Avenue.

■■■■■■

The next morning at Relax Sinsations, Monique bobbed into the place, just as merrily and gingerly as any giddy love struck young girl.

"Whass'up y'all?" she said, speaking to everyone and went speechless when everyone yelled Monique.

"Oh my God! When did y'all come home?"

"This morning," Chyna Doll spoke for her, Slim, Blondie, L.L. and Flame.

"Aaaaahhh!" they all screamed, and had a group hug in the middle of the parlor. When they separated, Tammy pulled Monique to the side.

"Baby, we need to talk," Tammy said to Monique.

"I'm all ears," Monique said.

Tammy pulled Monique into the office part of the parlor, and sat her down.

"Mo," she began, "I've been thinking a lot about what you said about us and making a decision. And I finally think I'm ready."

Monique was silent. She wasn't impressed by any of this hoopla. However, she did feel some guilt. But that wasn't her fault either. Had Tammy stopped bullshittin' and made the choice months ago, Monique would've probably never met Pretty E.

"Ready to make a decision to be with you," Tammy said proudly. *And after all the shit I put Pretty E through about messing with a white girl, here I go in love with one myself,* she thought, waiting on a response from Monique.

"Why did it take you this long to decide?" Monique asked.

"Because I wasn't sure."

"So, you're sure now?" Monique asked.

"I'm positive," Tammy said, and Monique lit up like a Christmas tree.

"Thank you, baby! Thank you! Thank you for choosing me," Monique replied, but only happy because she knew what was about to happen. "So, when will you tell him?"

"Tonight," Tammy said. "Soon as I'm able to go home and pack my shit."

When Monique was alone, she dialed Pretty E's number.

"Whass'up Reds?" Pretty E asked.

"It's done, baby. She made her choice," Monique said.

"Did you make yours?" he asked.

"You know I did."

"When will you be home?" he asked.

"When she walks out the door," Monique said.

"I heard dat."

"I love you, Daddy."

"And Daddy loves you back, Reds," and they hung up the phone.

# Chapter Twenty

The day was finally over, and Tammy was ready to get it over with. The time had come that she never thought would come. The time she would leave Pretty E. Her mind was made up, and Monique was who she was in love with. Now, the only thing left for her to do was do it. Go home, tell the nigga it's over, then pack her shit and leave. And now she was pulling up to the house. With her heart pounding, she mustered up the courage to go forth with it.

Pretty E was already ready for what was to come, because Monique had already let him know. Right now, he thought, Reds probably on her way over here with her clothes and shit. Then in came Tammy, she still wasn't one hundred percent sure she wanted to leave Pretty E, but when he still ignored her like he had been doing for the past few weeks, her mind was made.

"And you couldn't even say hi to me when I walked through the door. Now that's crazy, Eric. I had even contemplated on reconsidering a decision I made earlier today. Ha!" she laughed sarcastically. "The nerve of me." Pretty E just looked at her, and that pissed her off even more. And to think this was the man I was to marry, she thought. Almost in tears, and Pretty E's face showed not an emotion.

"That's why I'm leaving you today, Eric. Because you don't love me, I'm just convenient to you, dat's all!" she snapped, and stormed off.

When Tammy got upstairs to the master bedroom and began to pack, her heart was crushed. Pretty E hadn't even followed her upstairs to at least try and change her mind. So, as she slung what belongings she wanted into her Louis Vuitton luggage, her heart started to ease. Ease to the fact that she was making the right decision now, instead of regretting it too late.

Tammy took a step by step with luggage in tow, on her way out the house. Pretty E was sitting on the couch.

"So, you're not even goin' to say as much as bye to me?" she asked Pretty E.

"For what? You made your decision," he said.

"Just like dat, huh?"

"Just like dat. See Tammy, you's a selfish ass mutha-fucka. I learned that the other day the way you acted, knowing I was going through some'um about Dog. And here you had the unmitigated gall to act a fool cause a nigga ain't shown you no attention. Bitch, you's crazy! I'm kind of glad yo' ass is leaving," Pretty E said bluntly, his words like darts into her heart.

Tammy fell apart. Pretty E had cut her deeply, almost to the bone with words. Replaying what he had just said to her just seconds ago had made her see just how selfish she actually was. But she made a commitment. She'd be less than a woman if she turned back now. She grabbed the handles to her luggage and pulled them both behind her, their wheels easily rolling over the carpet and stopped at the door.

"Eric, I'm sorry. I'm sorry we couldn't make it," Tammy said, and opened the door to leave. "What are you doing here?" she asked Monique, who was on the other side of the door.

"What do you mean, what am I doing here? Monique asked with a fake puzzled look on her face.

"Just what I said," Tammy shot back.

"I'm moving in, that's what."

"What!" Tammy shouted at the answer.

"Just what I said; I'm moving in. He's my man now, and like Jill Scott said, 'Your getting in the way of what I'm feeling'," Monique said as she carried in her belongings and brushed by Tammy to get into the house. "Excuse me!" she spat, and ran into the arms of Pretty E.

"Hey, Reds!" she spoke, and they kissed passionately. It was out—they were no longer a secret.

Using her heel on the six-inch stilettos she wore, Monique kicked the door shut behind her as they listened to the sobs of a heartbroken woman on the other side of the door.

When the door slammed shut, all Tammy could do was cry. She let the handles go on both of her suitcases and collapsed into a fetal position right on top of the welcome mat as she watched her man be taken by yet another white bitch.

■■■■■■

All they heard was a car door shut and some tires peeling off in the streets.

"What da fuck was dat?" Jaquaan asked, blowing the purple kush from his mouth before jumping up to go to the door.

He looked through the peep hole but couldn't see due to the letter that was taped over the peep hole.

What is it?" O.D.B. asked as Jaquaan snatched the letter away from the door.

"This," Jaquaan said, as they read the letter:

*This is what we do to Moolies and Muttz*

*Signed,*
*Capelli Family*

And they knew just who was behind it--it was the boah, Lil' Frank.

"Whass in da bag?" Boog asked hesitantly.

"Open it," Jaquaan said.

"Hell no, nigga, you open it!" Boog said.

"You's crazy as hell," Jaquaan said.

"I'll open the mu'fucka," O.D.B. said, and reached down to untie the bag. "Oh shit!" he shouted, startled as he jumped back and out rolled Bolo's head. Jaquaan cried.

"It's on, nigga! It's mu'fuckin' on! Them crackers gotta go!" Jaquaan snapped, not knowing that this would start a war that would continue for the next three generations.

It would always be that way--the Capelli's vs. any offspring of Rasul, Dog, Hit-Man and Pretty E, until one of the sides raised the white flag in surrender.

# Chapter Twenty-One

Two months had passed since Dog's funeral, and still no retaliation. The streets began to whisper. It must have been true, Rasul and Pretty E had been overthrown as the street bosses and gangsta's that so many had become accustomed to knowing. There were some new sheriffs in town, and there names were Tommy Good and Mike Cottman.

So, with the swagger of Muhammad Ali, Tommy and Mike cruised through the city of Wilmington's streets as if they owned them. They talked more shit to niggaz now then ever before, and the people began to wonder. All that was happening to their reputation was uncharacteristic right now. Rasul and Pretty E would never stand for this type of disrespect, but they were, that's what shocked people the most. However, there were still many people who knew they hadn't heard the last from Rasul and Pretty E.

Rasul and Pretty E had heard all the rumors that were circulating through the streets, and that only fueled their fire more. But intellect over emotion was Rasul's motto. He'd never make a move in the game called life with brainstorming on every possible outcome that could take place. He knew had he done what the streets wanted, he'da been in jail by morning. The streets wanted

Tommy Good dead, because he had the entire city walking on egg shells.

Tommy and Mike were running a full court press constantly, and making every drug dealer in Wilmington pay taxes. Every side of town passed off to Tommy weekly, and they were more than ready for the pressure to be released. They silently hoped now, more so than ever before, that Rasul and Pretty E came to handle these young cannons.

"Yo man, I'm ready to handle these mutha-fuckas right now," Pretty E said to Rasul.

"Nah, not yet, baby boy. That's what mu'fucka's want us to do. Don't you be hearing the word on the streets? Niggaz think we soft, they think these niggaz, Tommy and Mike, got us shook," Rasul said.

"Nigga, the way we fell back, I'm beginning to think we softened up."

"Do you feel like you soft?" Rasul asked.

"Fuck no!" Pretty E said.

"Well, why is you worried about what people think? You know and I know that them niggaz is handled, don't you?"

"Yeah."

"Well, fall back. I'm still learning. Davita is schooling me on everything about these niggaz. These niggaz is untangled at every edge. It's going to be like taking candy from a baby when we kill them niggaz," Rasul said, making sense like he always did.

Pretty E just nodded is head. Rasul always made him see shit his way.

"A'ight. If you say so, Rasul. You ain't never said nuffin' wrong before," Pretty E said.

"Hell no I haven't, and I ain't either. Them niggaz is running out of time. They'll be dead real soon. Real, real soon," Rasul said, and in walked Davita.

"Baby, where's Bolo?" Davita asked, used to the dog meeting her at the fence.

"Out in the yard," Rasul said.

"No he's not. I walked around the whole house."

"Was the fence open?"

"No," she said.

"Well, where da fuck is he at then?" Rasul asked, puzzled because he knew he had put him out in the yard.

"I don't know," Davita said, and headed upstairs to the room.

Davita looked around her new room for the last two months and smiled. It had gradually taken on her touch, and slowly faded Tameeka's away. At first, she was scared to ask Rasul to move any of his ex-wife's belongings, but when she did, he was more than willing to oblige. That made her even more secure.

So, over the past few months, they had agreed on making the guest room downstairs a personal little museum for Tameeka. Everything Tameeka had ever possessed had been tagged, labeled and placed neatly in the room. Her pictures covered the walls like wallpaper, and Rasul would spray her favorite fragrance in the air whenever he entered the room. At first, that act in itself made Davita jealous, but after he explained to her that that was how he gained solitude within himself, she understood. She knew exactly what he was talking about because she too sometimes thought about her husband, the infamous Tommy Good.

■■■■■■

Rasul searched damn near the whole neighborhood for his dog, Bolo. Making kissing sounds and whistling while he searched, he was becoming more and more frustrated, because he knew something was fishy. Bolo wouldn't just walk off like that. Maybe my son took him with him, he thought, and was thinking about calling him up. No sooner than the thought crossed his mind, his cell phone was ringing…it was Jaquaan.

"Dad," Jaquaan said, in between sobs. "Come over here, please. I need to see you right now.

"Whass wrong, Jaquaan?" Rasul asked concerned.

"They…they…they killed Bolo!" he spoke, as he was overcome with emotion.

"What? Who?"

"The Capelli family," Jaquaan said, but Rasul found that hard to believe.

"Who?" Rasul asked again.

"The Capelli's. They supposed to be some mob ran by Frankie 'Lil' Frank' Maraachi the third. They be up in Lil' Italy and stuff."

"Is that right?" Rasul asked, the name Frankie Maraachi causing feelings inside him.

"Yeah."

"A'ight, I'm on my way there," Rasul said, and hung up. "Come on, Pretty E, we goin' to Vandever Avenue."

"For what?" Pretty E asked.

"The Capelli's are back."

■■■■■■

Once Rasul and Pretty E got to the house, Rasul called Jaquaan. "We outside," he said, and out popped Jaquaan, Boog and O.D.B, carrying a potato sack.

"Let me see," Rasul said, and Jaquaan handed him the letter first.

Then O.D.B. passed off the bag, and Rasul look in it in disbelief, hurt and shame. He felt as though he slipped again. Seeing Bolo's head, he asked for the rest of the body to lay to rest, but there was none. He'd have to just bury a head that's all.

He looked to his son and then to his partners and said, "Handle this." He didn't want to get involved, because he knew Sophia's son Lil' Frank was just a child...his son could handle that.

## Chapter Twenty-Two

Lil' Frank had been sending flowers to Kia's job all week long, and he hadn't heard from her to even know if she got them or so. So today he decided to deliver the bouquet himself.

Lil' Frank, like always, illegally parked right in front of Kia's job, the beauty saloon. She had been working at Che-Che's Shop now for the last year and a half. With his usual slow bop, he bopped himself up the steps and into the shop to see why Kia hadn't responded.

Hearing all the commotion in front of the shop, the people inside all rushed to the window to see what was going on. When they looked outside, they noticed a black Maserati parked dead center of the street holding up traffic.

"Who is this?" one of the ladies with a head full of curlers asked. "What? He thinks he's the president or some'um?"

*Oh my God!* Kia thought. "No he didn't," she said to herself, when she noticed that it was Lil' Frank. "What is he about to do?" she asked herself, as he walked into the shop.

"Hey everybody. How y'all doin'?" he spoke to everyone before turning his attention to Kia, who was trying to complete her client's head at her station. "Hey, Kia, how you doin'? I see you have been getting my messages," he said, looking around at all the flowers he sent her all week long, carrying some more to add to the collection. "So, why haven't you been calling me?"

"Because you know I mess with Boog. You had to see the way he acted that night. I'm sure you remember, because you was fightin' him," Kia responded.

"Fuck dat nigga, Boog. That nigga ain't me. He can't do for you what I can," Lil' Frank said, noticing all the women in the shop ease dropping on their conversation.

"But...but..." she tried to say.

"But what? What time do you get off?" he asked.

"At 7:00 o'clock," she said.

"I'll be out front," Lil' Frank said, and handed her the flower he had bought, then kissed her cheek. "7:00 o'clock," he said. "I'll be here," and he bobbed out the door. The women in the shop was in awe, and the questions begun as soon as he left.

"Ooooh, Kia, girl! Who was that?" her co-worker, Lisa asked.

"I know, girl, cause he was fine as shit," a client said.

"What? What is he mixed or some'um?" another one asked.

"No, he's Italian," Kia said, answering the question.

"Mmm, girl, that boy was sharp! If you don't want him, I'll take his sexy ass," another one said. Then they all rushed to the window when they heard the sirens.

Outside, they saw for the first time ever a white boy snap on the cops in a black neighborhood.

"What? What da fuck you want?" Lil' Frank snapped.

"Why are you parked in the middle of the street like this?" the officer asked.

"Cause my name is Lil' Frank, and I do what the fuck I want," he said, and jumped in his Maserati and pulled off. The people in the shop couldn't believe their eyes or ears.

"Girl, what da fuck is he into?" Lisa asked.

"I don't know, but I do know his cousin is Skinny Joey. Joey Merlino, the boss of the Philadelphia mob."

"Girl, dat nigga is in da mob," Lisa said excitedly.

"I don't think so?" Kia replied.

"I do, and girl you need to get wit' dat nigga if you know what I know."

"I heard dat."

■■■■■■

Seven o'clock on the dot, six forty-five to be exact, Lil' Frank was pulling up to Che-Che's Shop. Lisa, Tammira, Valonté and Pepsi, Kia's co-workers had all stayed behind to see if Lil' Frank was really coming back. And when they saw the Maserati pull up, they were just as excited for their girl as she was.

"Oooh, Kia girl, here he comes," Valonté said, as Lil' Frank approached the shop.

Lil' Frank strolled up to the door dressed in a State Property, short sleeve Dickie outfit that revealed his forearms, and the word "La Costra" on the right, and "Nostra" on the left. One leg on his pants was rolled up, something he always did. It was a reminder to him to keep one leg up on the competition at all times. On his feet were house shoes, ones similar to the ones "O-Dog" wore in the movie Menace to Society. His dark temple taper was revealed slightly from under the New York Yankee fitted cap he wore, and his diamond studded chain hung down to his navel, matching his huge pinky rings perfectly.

When he smiled, Kia noticed something for the first time, not only did he have twin dimples, but his whole bottom row of teeth were iced out.

"Hey Ma. You ready?" Lil' Frank asked, when he entered the shop.

"Yeah, here I come," Kia said, catching all the winks and yeah girls she got from her girls on the down low, when he wasn't looking.

Lil' Frank walked Kia outside to his car, which was, like always, parked illegally. Lighting up one of his Capone cigarettes, he walked her around to the passenger side, and opened the door for her to get in. Once she was inside, she leaned over and did the same for him, not because she was being courteous, but because she saw the line of cars forming behind them, and she wanted to avoid the embarrassment. By her doing that though had earned brownie points for her with Lil' Frank, because he knew now that she wasn't selfish.

"Where we goin'?" Kia asked, as Lil' Frank climbed into the car.

"To dinner, why? Aren't you hungry?" he asked.

"I could use a bite to eat, but why no boots or sneakers?" she asked, looking down at his feet.

"Oh, my house shoes? Because dinner will be served at my house," he said and pulled off.

■■■■■■

Kia's eyes widened when they pulled up to the luxurious condos that were just building down on Wilmington's Riverfront. I know he don't live here, she thought to herself in disbelief. These condos start at a million, she knew, but Lil' Frank pulled up to the security gate and stopped.

Pulling out his residence ID card, he placed it to the laser eye box on the pole at the entrance, and slowly the security gate began to slide open. He drove his car into the parking garage on the lower deck, and pulled into a space marked "Reserved 12B.

Lil' Frank, always having a way with the ladies, walked around the car to let Kia out, and led her into the lower level elevators. The doors shut behind them, and Lil' Frank pressed 12-B, and they were hoisted away. Ding sounded the elevator door as it swung open, and they got out on the top level of the condos.

These, on the upper deck, were the most expensive because they were penthouses, so Kia was even more impressed. He might be the mob, she thought, stepping out into the outside hallway. Even the hallway is hot, she thought, as she walked under the roof next to the railing on some of the plushest carpet she'd ever seen. Then, by just happening to stop and looking out over the railing, her breath was nearly taken away at the sight. Her once little city was building up beautifully around her, and was begging to take on the look of the Baltimore Harbor.

"Come on," he said, snapping her out of her trance. "Let's go inside."

Walking into the penthouse suite was really what blew Kia away. Lil' Frank's shit was more than elaborate, it was down right stunning. A huge, larger than life size picture/poster of Al Capone hung on the immediate wall of the entrance. Hanging next to that was a smaller photo. This one was of the "Babe" Babe Ruth.

As they broke the threshold of the condo, Kia began to smell some kind of sauce's aroma in the air, while still taking in all of the condo she was now standing in. Pictures of mob members, mob hits, and Old Blue Eyes "Frank Sinatra" and the "Rat Pack" hung all over the wall, while Italian leather furniture designed the living and dining areas of the condo. She gasped, but only because of how the dining table was set up. Beautiful red roses sat in a vase at the center of the table, while candles made the scene soft. The way he had left the balcony doors cracked, managed to allow a breeze to creep through, blowing the curtains and tickling the little flames on the candles, which made shows appear on the walls.

"Make yourself at home," Lil' Frank encouraged her, and walked off into the kitchen area, where the smell that now had her mouth watering came from.

She watched him every step of the way, and licked her lips sexually as he tossed his State Property top off of his back and onto the floor of the dining area.

*Mmmm!* she thought, as she stared at Lil' Frank's back, which some tattoo artist had made into what seemed to be memorial. The word "Pop-Pop" tattooed across his shoulder blades, and a slew of other mob affiliated pictures engraved in ink covered his back.

Kia followed him out to the kitchen, only to find him cooking himself. He tossed garlic, chopped onions, and huge sliced pieces of sausage, pepperoni, shrimp and meatballs into the sauce. Spaghetti and pasta sauce was one specialty that Lil' Frank took on because he possessed Pop-Pop Frankie's secret recipe book. *Impressive!*

Carrying two huge plates of spaghetti, Lil' Frank sat them down on each end of the already set table. He then walked back into the kitchen to retrieve a huge roll of Italian garlic bread and a bottle of red wine.

"Come on, let's eat. I'm starvin'," Lil' Frank said, pouring two glasses of wine.

"Me too. It smells delicious," Kia replied.

"I hope you like it," he spoke, and they sat down to eat.

- 153 -

Both digging into their plates, Lil' Frank really began to take on Kia's beauty. Her light complexioned skin and hazel brown eyes looked beautiful on her oval shaped face. With extension braids perfectly braided in her hair, she sorta looked like Alicia Keys, just Kia was more feminine then the megastar.

"Damn, dis bitch is really sexy," Lil' Frank said to himself, as she patted the corners of her mouth, then licked some sauce from her lips, sending a small tingle through his fuck stick.

Kia was just as mesmerized as him, as she stared in his direction. Lil' Frank's whole torso was completed covered with tattoos, nearly covering his chiseled little frame, but the shit was still sexy. Kia licked her lips. Lil' Frank was that nigga. And even though she knew she could never build a future with him, she wasn't going to lose the chance of having a one night escape of gut wrenching lovemaking and hardcore sex to ease her mind and body.

■■■■■■

When they were sure they had both had enough to eat, Lil' Frank began clearing the table. He carried the dishes to the already prepared dish water.

He was about to begin washing the dishes, but Kia came from behind him and said, "I'll do'em," turning Lil' Frank away.

Lil' Frank walked out into his living room and flopped down on the couch. He grabbed the remotes to both his 52-inch plasma, and On Demand cable shit, and went straight to Chris Brown's *On and Poppin'* video.

"Say, what yo name is?"

"Oooh, girl, that fits you girl," Lil' Frank began to sing along with the words. "It's the first time I had a girl whose looks set me on fire. I really want to get to know you better girl, you ain't gotta act like you shy," came from the kitchen as Kia sang along.

"Shorty kept it on and poppin'," Lil' Frank sung.

"Shorty keeps it on and poppin'," Kia finished the hook, and they laughed.

"Girl, you crazy," Lil' Frank said when she came out to where he was pasted before the television.

"So, whass'up? Do you dazzle all the girls with your charm?" Kia asked.

"Only the ones I like," he said.

"I must be one of them then."

"You're at my house, ain't you?" And as if reading each other's mind, they kissed and caressed each other where they stood.

It was odd at first for Kia, because her five nine frame, nearly six feet in heels, had caused her to bend down to kiss Lil' Frank, who stood five feet even. Lil' Frank knew that to be only a minor setback, because you're the same size in bed.

With that, he swept her off her feet and carried her into the bedroom. She was impressed at how his tiny frame compacted so much strength.

Lil' Frank peeled each piece of clothing Kia had on her body off one by one. It was like taking the skin off an orange with each peel, revealing just how juicy the treat was to become. When she was butt naked, Lil' Frank stepped back from the bed in admiration. Kia's body was perfect and her fuck hole was perfectly bold.

Mmmm, Lil' Frank went straight to work as his tongue flicked in and out of her soft spot rapidly, sending her into a fit of nerve ending shakes, before begging for the dick.

"Please put it in, Lil' Frank!" Kia whined, and found out that the rumor wasn't always necessarily true. Lil' Frank happened to be Big Frank where it counted most, as he jammed the snotty end of his fuck stick into her tiny little fuck hole, and banged away.

From the back, Lil' Frank grabbed a handful of extensions, and made his hand into a fist while placing the other one on her hip. Pulling slightly up on her extensions, caused her head to lift up like reigns would do a horse. And like a jockey in the Belmont Classic or Kentucky Derby, Lil' Frank rode her on across the finish line.

When they both reached their climaxes, something special happened to them. Nine months later, they'd be the parents of a one night stand. So as Lil' Frank drove Kia home the next morning, she hadn't the clue that in her uterus, hanging from her ovaries was the growing blood of true Las Costra Nostra...The Capelli Family.

## Chapter Twenty-Three

The next morning just so happened to be Friday, so to show his appreciation for a wonderful time last night, Lil' Frank woke Kia up.

"Hey pretty brown eyes, where'd you get those from?" he asked.

"From the milkman," she said, like an innocent child, but only she was playing and Lil' Frank cracked up laughing.

"Girl, you crazy as hell. Now that was crazy. The milkman, huh?"

"Learned it from my uncle. He taught me that when I was little to make my dad mad as a joke, because people always asked about my eyes. So he taught me the milkman. It used to burn my daddy up." She laughed at the memory.

"Damn, that's crazy. Well come on and get up. I want to do some'um for you to appreciate the time I had last night."

"Why? You did enough by cooking dinner," she said.

"That's nowhere nearly enough. Now come on before I change my mind," he teased.

Within the next ten minutes, she was up, had her teeth brushed and ready to go. The shower was taken last night. That's another thing that earned her brownie points with Lil' Frank. She had brought with her a change of undergarments and a toothbrush for the next day.

They reached the car, climbed in, and to City Line Avenue. Lil' Frank drove to Philly bobbing in and out of traffic as the V-12 engine dipped through traffic like a Ninja 1200. In no time they were at Sak's Fifth Avenue in the Chanel section, and Kia was modeling outfits. Finally agreeing on this one particular summer dress that was cut low, showing all cleavage, Kia was satisfied.

*Shit, it cost $1,250.00*, she thought, but Lil' Frank wasn't quite satisfied. He was after picking out a handbag, bracelet and matching Chanel necklace, and some Chanel clogs and frames, bringing the total cost for the one outfit to a whopping $4,800.00. Kia was beyond words.

"Want to drive back home so you can get to work?" he asked her, looking at her draped in Chanel from head to toe.

"Yeah, I'll drive," Kia said, and started the engine. She turned on the radio and their song was playing. In unison, they sung, "Shorty keeps it on and poppin'" Damn, why couldn't Boog be like this, she thought, minutes away from her job.

■■■■■■

Boog was parked out in front of Kia's job for nearly an hour now, and still no Kia. "She shoulda been here by now," he told himself madly, becoming more and more inpatient by the second. The only reason he was here was because he needed her apartment key.

He had left some coke over there the night before, and Jaquaan needed it for some nigga who was coming down from Chester. He was coming for five Kilos and two were at Kia's.

Mad, Boog started his car to leave, but noticed a car coming up in the rear. It was the Maserati of the boy Lil' Frank. What da fuck is dat nigga doin' over here, he thought, then soon found out, when Kia stopped in front of the shop.

"Nah, you straight. You ain't gotta find no parking spot, park this mu'fucka right here," Lil' Frank told Kia. "Right here in the middle of the street."

"You shouldn't do that all the time. One day the cops goin' to give you a ticket," Kia warned.

"And I'ma rip it up," he assured her.

Kia climbed from beneath the steering wheel after she cut on the hazards. "Hurry up and come around here and give me a hug before I go in here to this shop," Kia told Lil' Frank, as he stepped back away from the car, looking like she was straight from Hollywood, California. The all white Chanel dress, pocketbook, shoes and glasses had her looking like Sharon Stone in Basic Instinct. The white frames gave her a superstar look, while the fabric of the dress was so loose but form fitting on her that when the wind blew it, it blew the silk--almost satin material of the dress into the crack of her ass, revealing just how voluptuous she really was. Feeling a jam grow into her, she slid her freshly manicured nail hand behind her and pinched the fabric away. That was sexy in itself.

Lil' Frank bobbed around his car, gave her a hug and leaned her down toward him. On his tippy-toes, he reached up and kissed her lightly on the tip of the nose, and that sent Boog through the roof.

"Baby girl, I mean pretty brown eyes, you got my number, don't be afraid to use it for anything, anything at all. I'm always here for you, even when you don't see me," Lil' Frank said and pulled off.

Kia was gone. Boog needed to tighten his shit up. Tighten it up, and fast.

"Oh, so that's where you been," Boog stated sharply, startling Kia who was still staring at the brake lights on the car that sat at Vandever Avenue and Pine Street light.

"No," she lied.

"Oh, I see you in all new shit too, huh?"

"No, not really. This what I got on is new, but it's nothing special," she lied.

Not wanting to let her know that he was mad or worried, he simply said, "Let me see your keys so I can go get dat shit from out the house."

"Here. Oh, and baby, that's nothing. I told you he was my best friend in school," she lied again.

"I ain't thinking 'bout dat nigga," he lied, then silently told himself that the white boy, Lil' Frank, had to go. He took the keys and left without saying a word.

*So what*, she thought. *Boog won't spoil my day.*

■■■■■■

The Italian Festival, St. Anthony's Carnival, was a tradition for Wilmington's Italian section of the city, Little Italy. Every year in June on the fourteenth through the twenty-first, the festivities are in full stride from noon to midnight, and the first and last night of the festival was packed.

Today was Friday, though the last day would be Sunday. But by it being the beginning of the weekend, it was crowded more than it had been all week.

"Damn, I want me some funnel cake," Boog said, smelling the cake.

"Damn right. Let's get two of them mu'fucka's," Jaquaan said.

"Nigga, y'all better get three of'em, I want one too," O.D.B. said, as they made their way over to the food section of the Carnival.

That in itself had become a task, because every step that they took they stopped a different crew of young girls. The once five minute walk had turned into nearly a half hour journey from one part of the Carnival to the next.

Bells were going off, indicating that there was a winner somewhere at one of the water shooting games, Ferris Wheels spun, lights flickered off and on, bumper cars crashed and banged, and Carnival music filled the air as Lil' Frank and Fat Sal stood across from the funnel cake stand at the French fry stand.

They had been there mingling with the girls for mostly all of the night. The Carnival part of the festival had become old to them. They had outgroen the rides, but they'd sometimes do something else, like play skeet ball or shoot hoops to win stuffed animals. For now they were feeding their faces.

"Pass me that vinegar," Fat Sal said.

"And the ketchup," Lil' Frank said.

■■■■■■

Boog, O.D.B. and Jaquaan stood in line right behind some dude with a little boy and girl with him. They saw the guy when he first got up from the table with who was probably his wife. The way he was dressed, they knew he was probably a hustler, because he was dressed in Prada sneaks, D&G jeans and shirt, and his kids were dressed in Baby Phat and Rocawear. He knelt down to wipe some sugar from the funnel cake his son was eating that had gotten on his shirt away, and they couldn't help but notice the twin .45 caliber pistols that shoved in the small of his back.

Almost instantly they knew who the man standing in front of them was. His name was Mike Cottman. He was the only one with a reputation like that, the only man known to carry two .45s like that. So when he turned around and they saw that it was him, fear gripped them. Jaquaan lowered his head so he didn't make contact with Mike. The last thing he wanted to happen was for Mike to notice him, and realize he was Rasul's son. Then he'd surely be a dead man. But Mike paid them no mind. He never did any business when he was with his family.

"Hey, whass'up youngin's?" Mike spoke, brushing between the three of them.

"Whass'up," they all spoke back, and watched as him, his wife and kids left the Carnival.

"Yo, that was Mike Cottman," O.D.B. said in disbelief, as if he had just seen a superstar up close.

"Yeah, but there goes Lil' Frank," Jaquaan said, spotting him and Fat Sal by the French fry stand.

Boog's heart dropped, not from fear, but because he had a gut feeling that he was fuckin' his girl, Kia. Not to mention the way the fight ended. Boog still felt as though he lost the fight and wanted some get back.

"It looks like they by themselves," Boog said.

"No they not," Jaquaan said. "Look." He turned his head in every direction that he saw a young Italian. Then they realized that again they were outnumbered.

"Come on. I know what to do," Jaquaan began. "We goin' to have to ambush them niggaz. What time is it?"

"We got five minutes 'til this closes. Come on," O.D.B. said, and they left.

Lil' Frank noticed them the whole time they were there. He wanted to go tell Boog just how blazin's Kia's shot was to start some'um with them, but decided against it. He had made his move already, he was jut waiting now to see if they'd respond. If they didn't, Lil' Frank knew it would be a piece of cake to do what he had planned next to do…rob them at the house on Vandever Avenue.

■■■■■■

Boog, O.D.B. and Jaquaan had stationed themselves in an alley somewhere between 7th Street and 8th and Lincoln, each armed with hammer, high caliber ones at that. None of their pistols was less than a .40 caliber. The plan was to catch Lil' Frank off guard. Nothing was more surprising than the element of surprise. Not knowing what lied before you. So now as the people exited the Carnival by way of Lincoln Street, they anxiously waited for Lil' Frank to walk by on his way to his car.

Lil' Frank picked at his French fries one by one as Fat Sal followed in tow. Fat Sal, on the other hand, had a more difficult time trying to balance on a paper plate funnel cake, cotton candy, French fries, a couple of hot dogs, and a Italian water ice, all at the same time. Not to mention balance himself on one crutch, because of the leg shot he received at Bank-Shots that night.

Always protected by the New Capelli Family, Lil' Frank bobbed along. He was the new Don of what was to become the most powerful family the mob had ever seen. Camouflaged, the Family was spread about the crowd of ho homers like the measles. All with their eyes on the boss, Lil' Frank, and the under boss , Salvatore "Fat Sal" Terrango.

Jaquaan was the first to notice them approaching up the street. "Look, here they come," he told Boog and O.D.B. "This is what you do to Moolies and Muttz, huh?" Jaquaan said aloud, but to no one in particular, as they pulled the masks down over their faces.

Lil' Frank, always on point like an arrow, noticed the three mask men from out the corner of his eye and yelled, "It's a hit!" tackling Fat Sal to the ground as they rolled in between cars.

Boom! Boom! Boom! Boom! The barrage of gunfire exploded, causing a frenzy to take place, as bullet holes ripped through car doors and shattered car windows. Lil' Frank wasn't hit though, nor was Fat Sal.

Then another barrage of gunfire emerged, only this time from his Familia. He could tell by the auto-matchness of the weapons. The sound was no longer "Boom", it was "Tat-tat-tat-tat-tat" or "Pop-pop-pop-pop", and Boog, O.D.B. and Jaquaan took cover. They had been outmatched again, and chased away again.

Lil' Frank's cell phone rang. "Speak," he answered.

"Boss, they left in a SL 500 Benz," Sammy said from the other end, and Lil' Frank formed a smile. It was confirmed, he knew exactly who was behind this.

"Fat Sal, you alright?" Lil' Frank asked his friend of a lifetime, while shaking broken glass from his wife beater T-shirt.

"Yeah, I'm alright," Fat Sal said, then began to snap. "Goddamn it! Those mu'fucka's," he said.

"What, Sal? What happened?" Lil' Frank asked, worried.

"Those mutha-fuckas made me smash my funnel cake!" he answered, peeling the funnel cake off of the seat of his pants.

Lil' Frank laughed his ass off.

■■■■■■

Davita told Rasul and Pretty E that Tommy picked up money from one of his workers every Friday night on 30th and Market Street, and tonight would be no different. The only difference was that this time, Rasul and Pretty E would be waiting right there...right there on 30th and Market Street. It was settled; Tommy Good and Mike Cottman would die right there.

■■■■■■

Rasul and Pretty E parked their cars on 28th and Tatnall, right behind the project apartment building and got out. They greeted each other, then walked to their destination spot. The spot, the alley behind the old West Coast Video Rental spot directly across from Kennedy Fried Chicken. Dressed in black, Rasul and

Pretty E stepped back into the darkness of the alley, not visible to the naked eye and waited.

"Dog, this one's for you," Rasul said, looking up to the stars.

■■■■■■

*"Say Hi Zavvy, Hi Mommy,*
*Everybody say Hi to Armani.*
*She so beautiful,*
*She my Booda Boo,*
*You say anything it's gotta be*
*She Cutie Cute..."*

The sounds of Delaware's own Pretty Thugger, Mr. Ira Bland, exploded through the speakers of Tommy Good's GT Bently.

"Yo, this boah is hot!" Tommy yelled to Mike, who was in the passenger seat.

"I know. He from Concord Avenue, ain't he?" Mike asked.

"Yeah, this shit hot though. It's a song for his daughter. Makes me think about my Booda Boo, cause she definitively Cutie Cute," Tommy spoke of his five-year old daughter.

"Mines too," Mike added. "I know this money better be straight this week, cause if it's not, I'ma shoot this mu'fucka's hand."

"Yeah, foot or some'um," Tommy added.

"Fuck it, I might as well kill his punk ass. Then the rest of these bitch niggaz will know what time it is," Mike stated.

"It depends on how short." Tommy showed compassion.

"Not a penny short, nigga. Nigga better look on the ground and pick one up," Mike said seriously.

"Man, you crazy as hell," Tommy said, stopping at the red light on 30th and Market.

Tommy turned on his left blinker, so he could park right in front of the store, and waited patiently for the traffic to resume.

"It's now or never. Let's leave these mu'fucka's slumped right here in their pretty ass Bentley," Pretty E said and was off.

"Let's go," Rasul said.

The light turned green, but the van in front of them was turning so, so they had to wait for the oncoming traffic to pass by. That gave Rasul and Pretty E perfect opportunity, as they ran up on the Bentley. Rasul ran to Tommy's side, the driver side, and Pretty E to the passenger side. They both raised their .357 revolvers and aimed them into the direction of the windows. The Queen in this game of chess, Davita had set up a perfect checkmate.

Tommy looked through his side view mirror and saw the attack coming, his heart dropped. He tapped Mike on the leg and made him aware of what was about to become. Mike laughed. Tommy looked for an out, but there was none, they were caught in traffic.

Damn, Tommy thought. Then to not show any signs of fear, they looked at their attackers straight in the face and smiled. Rasul and Pretty E couldn't believe their eyes.

They raised their pistols and Boom! Boom! Boom! shot at their victims. Tommy and Mike laughed as hard as they ever had before at their attackers. The Bentley's windows were bulletproof. It wasn't a checkmate after all. Rasul and Pretty E were dumbfounded. They had just realized how far out of touch they were, as Tommy sped off, leaving about thirty feet of skid marks on the streets. Then the screams began.

"Oh my God!" a female's voice screamed at the top of her lungs.

"Nooooo!" another one screamed.

"Shaunté! Oh my God! Shaunté! Please! Noooo!" another one cried, as Rasul and Pretty E looked back over their shoulder and saw a shattered Kennedy Fried window, and a crowd forming outside.

It must've been bad they thought, hearing sirens off in a distance, so they bailed out, leaving the scene immediately.

One of the bullets from Rasul's gun had ricocheted off of Tommy's window and shot back through Kennedy's. The bullet pierced through the window, shattering it and hit the young girl in the upper chest, in which she was bleeding profusely. Her upper body still laid in the store, while her bottom half, legs and feet, were out on the entrance doorsteps.

Two days fresh from graduating Howard High School, she was to lose her life. That's just how shit happened in the 'hood…here today and gone tomorrow.

∎∎∎∎∎∎

Tommy Good and Mike Cottman had escaped death's clutches yet another time, and were leaving an ambush unharmed. Tommy pulled over to the side of the god, got out still laughing and high fived Mike across the roof of his car. He walked around to the front of his Bentley and dropped to his knees, opening his arms wide as if to hug the car, and did just that.

"My baby," he said, proudly kissing the symbol on the 'hood.

Tommy's Bentley was redone with so much Teflon and titanium, that a bomb from Omar Khadafi wouldn't have harmed them. Retaliation was a must. Rasul and Pretty E were walking dead men in the eyes of Tommy and Mike, but it wouldn't be that easy. Rasul and Pretty E were two savvy veterans that at any time, could strike again. This they knew, so they'd play it safe and step with caution.

## Chapter Twenty-Five

Detective Cohen was irate. He couldn't believe that someone had the audacity to shoot up a public landmark such as the Italian Festival. But this shit had to stop. The youngsters in this city were going absolutely crazy. They had turned the City of Wilmington, Delaware into "Hellaware". It was hell everywhere you went. Even now he was at a loss. He had the slightest idea who, why, or what happened here tonight. Just a whole lot of shell casings, riddled cars and broken glass. Then it hit him....this had to be the work of Lil' Frank and the new Capelli's. He'd dig into it more later.

Detective Cohen hadn't even fully left the Hill Top section of the city yet before dispatch came over the CB system in his unmarked squad car. "Calling all cars, calling all cars on the Northside section of the city. There's been reported gunshot fire at the corner of 30th and Market Street. There's been one wounded in what now has just been report a 187." And that's all Detective had to hear, he hit the button on his dashboard, causing the lights in the car's grill to come to life as he sped off towards the scene.

■■■■■■

Two hours hadn't even passed yet, and the entire city had heard the news of the failed assassination on Tommy Good and

Mike Cottman. They were glad to know, the majority was anyway, that someone had finally tried to get at the boahs, Tommy and Mike. They were upset to know they missed. They knew now for sure that Tommy and Mike were going to run pressure, more pressure than ever before.

When the news first started to circulate, the streets already knew who was behind the whole thing. It was Rasul and Pretty E. They just couldn't believe that they had missed their targets. That was uncharacteristic of them to do something and not pull through. That's what raised the question, are Rasul and Pretty E really washed up? Are they really has beens? The people would know soon enough, because they knew this wouldn't be the last of Tommy Good and Mike Cottman.

Davita saw the look on Rasul's face when he came home. She knew by the way he was looking that something had went down, and a sense of joy overcame her. It was done. Her brother could finally rest in peace. Rasul had killed Tommy. He probably don't want to break the news to me this way, Davita thought, looking into his eyes. He don't know it's going to be the happiest day of my life.

"Are you okay, baby? Here, sit down," Davita began. "Did you handle your business?"

"Yeah, but we," he paused. "We missed."

"What?" Davita asked shocked, and knew that Rasul was a dead man. She shoulda never involved him in her mess, but now it was too late.

"We missed," he said.

*But he won't*, she thought. Tommy and Mike had signed a deal with the devil.

■■■■■■

When Detective Cohen arrived at 30th and Market Street, it was a frenzy. He leaped from the car and walked over to where the paramedics were still working on the victim. His heart instantly went out to the parents of the victim, who couldn't be no more than seventeen years old.

*Damn!* Detective Cohen thought sadly. Then the question of why was she out so late proposed itself. He quickly put two and two together when he found the fake ID on her, and finished questioning her friends. Apparently they had just come back to Delaware from a club up Philly called Transit. The twenty-one and older club had been turned out itself, and they had barely escaped gunfire up there.

"I guess lightening does strike twice," the detective told himself, before wrapping up. "I guess it really does."

■■■■■■

Tammy hadn't been the same since Monique slammed the door shut with her foot on her that day, and that was weeks ago.

Every single day since that happened Tammy had cried tears of agony and betrayal. She had even went to see a psychiatrist about the depression she was experiencing. Snow White, Chyna Doll, Flame, L.L., Slim and Blondie all kept in contact with her daily, trying to feed her strength. See, they were Ho's at heart, the strongest women on the planet, and couldn't' be broken by anything. To them men were money…they came and went. They tried to explain that to Tammy, but she'd never see it that way. She wasn't a ho.

They all were a little mad at Monique at first, but they knew the game…it was cop and blow. Monique hadn't done a thing wrong, she simply saw opportunity and seized it.

"She got that one," Tammy said to herself, as she got dressed to go out.

Snow White had convinced her to put on a come fuck me dress and go out to a club or bar or some'em. Live again, be daring. Go out and suck and fuck some strange dick or some'em. Snow White had encouraged her. Yeah, I think I will go out, but suck and fuck some'em strange was out of the question.

Tammy looked in the mirror, giving herself her last once over. Satisfied, she headed for the door. "I'm going to the Safari Bar and Lounge," she said to herself. The Safari on Lancaster Avenue and Franklin Street was a nice laid back spot to chill. Usually packed, tonight it was comfortable. It wasn't all wall to wall stocked and uncomfortable with people. The reason why was because they were having a birthday party over the Tavern for deceased 'hood legend, Kenny "Love" Davis over South Bridge.

Tammy stepped into the Safari by herself, which felt odd. She never came out alone, so tonight she felt kind of naked. Then she missed Tameeka. It had always been since high school, Tameeka and Tammy. Now it was just Tammy. Walking into the Bar and Lounge, she let her eyes roam throughout the joint. She had seen some faces that she seen before, but none that she recognized as a hung out partner or anything like that.

Then she heard, "Tammy, girl, is that you?"

Tammy looked to the last booth and table in the back, the one by the dance floor and DJ booth and saw Tish, Rayon and Tasheena. Her face lit up.

"Hey, bitches," Tammy said, sliding in next to Rayon at the booth.

"Whass'up girl? How you been?" Tish asked.

"I been alright. How you been? Where's Kia? And when did you get back to Delaware?" Tammy asked Tish.

"Girl, I been fine. The wives of the N.B.A. have been a big support to me. In fact, the kids are with those Kobe Bryant's wife now. She's keepin' them while I go through this appeal thing with my husband, Trans. It's looking good, he should be home by Christmas, and girl, I can't wait." Tish said excitedly.

"Oh, that's whass'up."

"Whass'up wit' you and Pretty E?" Rayon asked.

"Girl, that nigga done left me for another white bitch," Tammy said, causing a shocked reaction.

"Get da fuck outta here!" they all said in unison.

"Girl, and did."

"That's fucked up, girl. I always thought you was too good for that nigga anyway," Rayon said.

"Now what you goin' do? You goin' to get to know Allah or what?" Tasheena asked, not in total Hijab, but wore a Kemar.

"That's probably what I need."

"That is what you need," Tasheena assured her.

"Girl, we came out to have a nice time. We didn't come to hear you preach," Rayon said, sipping her Apple Martini.

"I just see a sista in need, dat's all. But Allah is Akbar," Tasheena said, sipping her straight cranberry on the rocks.

For the next couple of hours, they sat together at the table getting reacquainted with one another, while checking out the men. Then in walked Tommy Good.

■■■■■■

Tommy Good paid his ten dollars at the door, stepped in, then looked the bouncer dead in the eyes like, *I wish you would pat me down, nigga!* The bouncer got the message loud and clear. Tommy brushed by him, and walked into the belly of the club, nearly snatching the air out the room. The people inside the club looked on as if they were seeing a ghost, remembering what they heard just hours ago. And in this little city that always happened. Mutha-fucka's always got the story wrong.

The way they heard it, Tommy and Mike was dead, but that was the most bullshit story ever. Tommy was alive and here in the flesh, dressed in a body fitting Dolce Gabbana shirt. Tommy's upper body looked like that of Tyrese's in the movie Baby Boy. On his legs were D&G jeans also. He wore D&G sneaks too. Tommy looked like a model, and the women were taking notice. The first was Tasheena.

"See, now if I was still doin' me, I'd be all over his ass," Tasheena said, then said, "Y'all want to have fun, don't you." And they laughed.

"Girl, you crazy as hell," Tish said.

"No I ain't. Y'all can't say he ain't sharp."

"He is sharp," Rayon said. "But do you know who that is?"

"Who is it?" Tammy asked.

"That's Tommy Good," Rayon told them.

"Not Lil' Tommy Good from over the Eastside," Tish said.

"Yeah, that's him," Rayon assured them.

*But he looked nothing like the way he did at the funeral,* Tammy thought.

"I remember he was a dirty lil' boy," Tish said.

"Well, he ain't dirty now," Tasheena said.

"He sure ain't," Tammy added, then wondered why and how a brotha that looked so good could be so damn menacing.

Tommy noticed the women at the back table diggin' him. So after he ordered his double shot of Remy Martin with his trademark one ice cube, he sent to their table a bottle of Yellow Rosay by the bartender.

"Classy," they agreed, as he made his way over to their table.

"Well hello, ladies, "Tommy greeted them. "May I sit down with y'all?"

"I ain't goin' to get shot, am I?" Tasheena teased.

"You might," he answered with a smile, but was dead serious. And by me at that, he thought. Smart bitch.

Then Tommy turned his attention to Tammy. Damn, she looked familiar as hell, but he didn't say nothing. Then like a light bulb clicking on in the cellar, he remembered where he saw her from…the funeral sitting next to Pretty E.

"Tammy, right?" he asked.

"Yeah, that's me. How'd you know that?"

"Let's just say we have someone in common."

"Oh, I see."

"Yeah, we can talk somewhere," she responded, scared to death. She ain't know whether to run, say no, or call the cops and tell.

But when he spoke, she got a different vibe from him, a warm one at that. She couldn't see in him all that people said about him.

"Is Pretty E your man?" he asked.

"Was my man." Then it hit her. This was her time to get some get back.

*Check,* Tommy thought, regaining power on the chessboard of life by capturing their Queen to even the game.

"Was, huh?" he asked, and for the rest of the night they vibed. The liquor made her talk more.

## Chapter Twenty-Six

Rasul sat in the day room of his home, the one that had become a museum for Tameeka, and tried to make sense of this whole mess. Holding daughter in his arms as she slept on his chest made him re-evaluate some shit in his life.

She was the most important thing in the world to him right now…her and Jaquaan. Maybe it was time to step down, let the reigns go and pass off the torch. Rasul would be a fool to continue to jeopardize everything he had accomplished and gained from the streets over the years.

Besides, Tommy and Mike were, to Rasul's surprise, a lot smarter than he gave them credit to be. They were borderline brilliant, had the heart of lions and youth. They were what the streets had become since they first started in their era. Today's game was more deadly than when he played it, and Tommy and Mike set the standard.

*Yeah, I think I'ma be done,* Rasul thought. However, he quickly started to change his mind. He was Rasul. "Fuck if I'm going to let some loose cannon of a young boy scare me off. I set the standard in this shit. Fuck a Tommy and a Mike. I'ma kill them mu'fucka'!" Rasul shouted, scaring the baby awake. "I'm sorry, booda boo. These niggaz think daddy soft, that's all," he said, and stood to his feet. "Dog, I ain't goin' out like dat," Rasul said, looking at the picture of them when they were kids on field day. "You know that, don't you?"

■■■■■■

The next day, Rasul was up bright and early. Today was their wedding anniversary. It woulda been five years today. So, as he got dressed and kissed Davita on the cheek, he began to feel odd. Something just wasn't right. He walked outside and decided that today he would drive the Jaguar instead of the normal…the Benz.

Rasul flicked through pages of this CD case until he found it. His Raphael Sadiq CD. He turned it to the song he wanted as the soft sounds of It's Our Anniversary began to play softly but loudly through the car's system.

Rasul pulled up to Gracelawn Memorial Cemetery and parked on the road in front of where his wife was buried at. He opened the door, pressed repeat and turned the radio all the way up.

"Tomorrow will come, and girl, I can't wait, it's our anniversary," he sung with the music, as he danced in front of the tombstone.

■■■■■■

Tammy's information had been precise. She told them that Rasul would be at the cemetery bright and early on their anniversary day. And there he was, dancing with some flowers in front of her tombstone. They came from out of the hiding spots just a few feet away from where Rasul's wife was buried. They had been sitting down with their backs up against the tombstones they decided to hide behind since the gate first opened. That's what made them so special, they knew patience was the best thing a man could have, and it was about to pay off.

■■■■■■

Rasul sung with his eyes closed and danced his heart away, caressing the flowers as if they were Tameeka herself. Oh, how he missed his wife. There was even some days when he wished someone would blow his brains out so he could get to her faster. There were others when he didn't. Today was like that. It was one of those days in which he wished he could die so he'd get to see her again. Not knowing that the saying, be careful what you wish for, cause you just might get it, was true.

■■■■■■

Tommy and Mike crept across the grass towards Rasul with their guns down around their sides. Tip-toeing, they stepped lightly and were now only a few feet away from him. They raised their pistols.

Rasul felt as if he was being watched, but that's just how cemetery's made you feel. They always made you feel like you was in the presence of someone else at all times, probably was the spirits, that's why Rasul never turned around. With his eyes still shut, him singing at the top of his voice, and dancing endlessly, the last thing in the world he visualized was Tameeka's smile.

*Checkmate!* Tommy thought, as his Queen, Tammy, had put him in position. Checkmate, he thought again.

Looking at each other in the eyes before they squeezed the triggers, they smiled. It was just that easy. They remembered what Skip told them the night they killed Hollywood.

"Yo, like Sha-rock used to say, 'caught'em slippin'"

Pop! Pop! the shots sounded, just two of them--one from each of their guns, and Rasul crumpled. Falling in what seemed to be slow motion, he hit his knees first, then he fell flat on his face right on top of his wife's grave.

The scenes from his life flashed through his mind as he began to feel faint and go in and out of consciousness. His breathing began to slow, his heart rate dropped, and his eyes were rolling up in the back of his head. He tried to focus them. When he did, the last thing in this world he saw was: Our Mom, My Wife, Our Friend, Tameeka Johnson. They'd be together forever now, from now to eternity.

*Street Knowledge!*
*"So Real You Think You've Lived It!"*

# The Rise And Fall of

## The Capelli Family

## And

## Frankie 'Lil' Frankie' Maraachi, III

# Chapter One

## The Meaning of La Costra Nostra

Frankie Maraachi was born in the homeland of Italy, as the Italians called it, on January 1, 1935. Coming from the poverty stricken part of Sicily, from a father who was a carpenter, and a mother who was a baker, Frankie hadn't grown with much of a childhood because he was forced to work with his father at a young age. So learning responsibility was imbedded in the kid at the tender age of nine years old. No play and work all day was all Frankie remembered about the Old Country, because soon after his ninth birthday, his father had gotten a job in the States…the United States of America.

The day Frankie and his family set sail from Italy to the USA, was the most exciting day of him and his little sister, Maria's life. The land of milk and honey was now going to be their home. Frankie was amused. He was going to the USA, to the big city…New York. All he could think about was the New York Yankee's, a guy named Babe Ruth and Joe "Mr. Coffee" DiMaggio. Not to mention Mickey Mantle. Maria, on the other hand, wanted to be a movie star and live in Hollywood, California. They both were a little disappointed when they got to the first state of all the twelve colonies…Wilmington, Delaware.

The house their parents had moved into was a gift from his father's new boss. To Frankie and Maria, the house was like a mansion. It looked like the house in the new movie, Gone With The Wind, and for the first time in their lives, they had their own rooms. The house itself was in a section of Wilmington that was known as "Little Italy" because it was where all the Italians had come to migrate.

"Wow!" they said together, as they ran through the house, and Frankie knew then he'd never have to work again.

His mother and father were even more astounded than the kids were. It was a big step up from the two bedroom shack they had moved from in Italy. Frankie's father was sure to progress in the land of milk and honey now, if this was his start. There was no place to go but up.

Frankie's father's name was also Frankie. He was an honest man, and a hard worker who had caught the eye of his new boss, Carlo Mirando, from the states. He was into building houses, apartment complexes, playgrounds, and whatever else was in demand, and he loved Frankie's work so much he asked him to join him in the states. Frankie agreed, and here he was, tomorrow would be the first day at work.

"Baby, the house is beautiful," Frankie's wife, Sophia said.

"Yes, very," Frankie responded, with a warm embrace.

"Frankie, I love you."

"You too, Sophia, I love you too," Frankie said.

2

Sophia was the love of Frankie's life. He had met her at a church festivity one Sunday. They were teens at the time. Frankie, being poor and living in the shacks, was still a handsome guy. Handsome enough for Sophia to catch an interest in him. Her parents, though, despised young Frankie and forbid Sophia to see him.

See, they were rich and well off. The last thing they wanted was for their beautiful little angel to be seeing someone whose future held nothing more than what he already had...nothing.

So they constantly warned her, "If you see that guy named Frankie from church, you will be disowned as a daughter to us. He isn't up to our standard."

"But Father."

"There's no but Father, there's only what I said." And Sophia hated him for that. She also hated her mother for not standing up for her. So now, to make them eat those words, she ran off with Frankie to the shacks, only to give birth to a baby girl, Maria.

From that day forth, Sophia had been disowned, and never regretted a day of it. Yeah, she missed the money, but she'd rather be broke and living in shacks then to be rich and unhappy.

■■■■■■

Carlo Mirando's Construction Company had earned a good name for themselves, as fair priced for top quality building. They had enough contracts to last for the next few years, something almost unheard of. How they got all those contracts was unknown to most, but not to all. See, Carlo had ties, ties to "La Costra Nostra", the Mafia.

Being affiliated with the Columbo's was a major plus for him. The Columbo's, one of the five families out of New York City, would come down and muscle other construction companies away from biding prices for the jobs that were needed, and Carlo would get them…it was just that easy.

Only thing he had to do was pay the Columbo's a percentage off of every job. Sweet, huh? But not always. See, by becoming affiliated with the Mafia, you're protected by every angle of the matter. You were nearly untouchable. The police even second guessed bothering a operation they knew to have mob ties. The only disadvantage you had was that at anytime they can turn on you, and muscle a business right from underneath you if you didn't abide by the rules. But Carlo always did. He enjoyed the luxuries of being untouchable, and the mob had made it that way.

"La Costra Nostra", the Mafia was started out in the homeland on Old Country, as it was often called by a group of men who wanted to protect the neighborhood from anything that would wart harm to it. So they would meet secretly and do things for the community that even the police or government wouldn't do. If a family was hungry, they'd feed them, if they were robbed or mugged, they're items would be returned surprisingly, and in the

4

case of a financial matter, it would be taken care of. That's why the people ran to these guys instead of the law, because they cared.

The Mafia, or "La Costra Nostra" had spread over into the United States in major cities...Chicago and New York to be specific. In Chicago, you had Al Capone, and in New York, you had Lucky Luciano. But after the Valentine's Day Massacre in Chicago, orchestrated by Al Capone, the world received the message. It was better to join them, then go against them, and Al Capone had earned by this single event the name of the Greatest Mobster, and Public Enemy Number One. But still, he was untouchable.

It didn't take long for Frankie Maraachi to notice the affiliation his new boss had with the mob, but he wanted no parts of it. He stayed away and minded his own, done his job, and went home. Years later, he would probably be turning over in his grave to know that his son, Frankie Maraachi, Jr., would become the boss of a family called "The Capelli's". He probably sat up when he found out his grandson would become the most feared, the richest, and the most hated by law enforcement agencies of all time. Frankie "Lil' Frank" Maraachi the III...that was "La Costra Nostra".

■■■■■■

# Chapter Two

## Starting A Family

From as far back as Frankie, Jr. could remember, he always had an attraction for the gangsters. Although his father was an honest man, and his mother was a hard worker, and together the two of them had never shown him and Maria anything other than the right way, the United States had showed him different. The gangsters and mobsters were the ones who seemed to be having all the success. They were everywhere; on television, in the newspapers, the magazines, the radio, everywhere. And even though people knew who they were and that they did, they were still accepted as "good people" amongst the locals. That's what attracted Frankie.

Frankie loved his new neighborhood like nothing else he could think of loving before. From the smell of the fresh bread baking at the bakery his mother worked at on 8th and Scott Street, to the fish market on 9th and Lincoln. Frankie loved running straight out the door after school to accompany his new friends, Ricky and Nicky Stango, Joey Vito and Lenny Ionni, then running down to either one of those spots to help out. Mainly the bakery, because more times than none, they were paid with fresh pastries of some sort. The fish market usually paid with change of some sort, sometimes more than others.

6

Ricky and Nicky Stango were twins that looked nothing alike, something they liked, because they had individuality…they weren't just known as the twins. Joey Vito was an only child at the time, but was real sly and sneaky, which later in life gave him the title "The Fox", and Lenny Ionni was a huge guy from the day they met. Not hugely muscular or anything like that, but fat as hell. He was huge that way, and even at age nine and ten, his shoe size of twelve had outgrown him by that age. They always teased him about that.

The five of them, Joey, Ricky, Nicky, Lenny and Frankie were inseparable…they did everything together. From playing stick ball, to popping the fire hydrants, to going down to this little bar called Lil' Italy on Sunday's, to wash the mobsters cars, and look at all the pretty women. Lil' Italy was their favorite pastime.

Lil' Italy was located only blocks away from where Frankie lived, but right across the street from Ricky and Nicky's house. The place had been off limits to them by their parents because they knew it was the hangout for local wise guys and mob members. The family in Delaware was a branch off of the Columbo's family tree, but still they were mob. Frankie and the crew loved them. They walked liked them, talked like them, acted like them, dressed like them and everything, quickly catching the attention of Carlo Mirando, Frankie's father's boss.

"Hey, aren't you Frankie Maraachi's kid?" Carlo asked one day, accompanied by one of the beautifullest women they'd ever seen, and apparently drunk off of something.

"Yes, Mr. Mirando," Frankie replied hesitantly.

"Does your father know you're down here?" he asked sternly, looking Frankie, Jr. in the face.

"No," he answered truthfully.

"Well, he still don't," Mr. Mirando said, and peeled from a knot of money he held a twenty dollar bill. "That's for you and your friends."

"But Mr. Mirando, it's five of us. This is only a twenty dollar bill. Now five more dollars would do us straight, that way we'll all have five dollars a piece," Frankie, Jr. said. It was gutsy, and caused for a lot of heart, but he did it anyway, and Mr. Mirando loved it.

"Here you go," he said, peeling another twenty instead of a five. "Here, now y'all got eight dollars a piece. Frankie, way to be loyal, it'll take you a long way in life. A real long way," Mr. Mirando said, before walking away, and Frankie and the crew were in disbelief.

"Man, Frankie, you really had balls to do that," Joey said.

"I know, man. You asked for more money after he had already given you a twenty for us," Lenny said.

"Tell me about it. I thought he would say that that was ungrateful or something," Ricky added.

8

"I thought he was going to take it back," Nikki stated, but all were still amused.

It was that day that would earn Frankie respect, and the recognition as the smartest of the crew. They'd for the rest of their lives follow Frankie's judgment on any and everything he set out to do. It was the making of a family, "The Capelli Family".

## Chapter Three
### Wise Guys

A "wise guy" was a term used by the mob to describe men who were affiliated with the mob, but not made men. Actually, they were more like pledge members in a fraternity or something. They mostly did all the foot work. Made men would often bring a well known, stand up guy type of wise guy with them when it was time to open the books for new members, in hopes that they'd be accepted.

Nine times out of time, they were shot down the first time like convicts coming up to the parole board, but they were eventually granted membership soon after. Wise Guys were the ones who put in all the foot work, from running pressure on local stores, to hijacking liquor trucks, freight trains, and other business that needed handling...the wise guys were the ones to do it. It seemed like to Frankie and his crew that the wise guys had more fun than anyone else, so that's what they started to imitate.

Frankie was almost fifteen now and nearly out of high school, when the mob began to take serious inquiries about Frankie and his crew. To Michael, the head of the Columbo's in Delaware, these five youngsters were making quite a bit of noise around the neighborhood, and he wanted to meet them. And meet them he did.

One afternoon, while walking home from school, Michael Sirroni saw the five of them entering a small hardware store, and leaving with a brown envelope. Once down the street, he watched as Frankie started passing out the money. Not knowing what was going on, Michael rolled up on the bunch, catching them off guard.

"Whass'up? What are you's guys doin' here?" Sirroni asked.

"Nothing, Mr. Sirroni," Frankie lied.

"Don't lie to me. Now, what is it that you's were doin'?" he asked again. "Or do I gotta take you's back into that hardware store and find out myself."

"No, Mr. Sirroni. Well, see, it's like this...everyday, like today is our collection day. We collect money from a couple stores weekly to keep them from being vandalized by neighborhood thugs and stuff. But in reality, we're the thugs. So really, their just paying us to leave'em alone. Smart, huh?" Frankie said, with a smile.

"Smart it is," Michael said. "But why are you robbing your own kind blind? Take your asses down to some of th black stores, super market groceries stores, or Spanish stores, rob them mu'fuckas!"

"But..."

"But nothing. If you could rob your own, you can rob them. Now where's my share?" Michael said, arm extended towards Frankie and palm up.

11

Frankie fidgeted at first from all the nervousness of handing Mr. Sirroni some money, but he felt more than privileged to be giving a known mobster some money.

"Here, how about this?" Frankie made the split, leaving everyone sixty dollars apiece.

"So it was $360.00 in all?" Michael asked. "What if I wasn't here?"

"Then we'd all have seventy-two, not sixty," Frankie said. Michael smiled.

■■■■■■

Since that run in with Michael as they were leaving the hardware store, they had been hanging out at Lil' Italy's Bar & Lounge more often than none, and the locals began to take notice, often running back behind Frankie's back and the rest of the crews to tell their parents. It seemed that none of the parents cared, except for Frankie's.

I guess from them being actually from the Old Country, they wanted to lead by example, show the people of the states that you could make it earnest with a little hard work. The rest of the crews' family didn't care one way or the other. They were raised in the states, and found out that organized crime was the American way. So, by them being down at the mob's hang out spot was more of a benefit than a liability.

They started off light at first, knocking a few tractor trailer's off, then moved on to the big stuff...the jewelry stores and freight trains, and Michael Sirroni, boss of the Delaware Columbo's, loved their work. They were no nonsense at all times, but when they pulled the hit off on a local rat for Mr. Sirroni, they were more than showered by the mob members, they were respected as stand up guys. And that's what wise guy did, and Frankie and his crew were the best wise guys of'em all, at the tender age of sixteen.

# Other Novels

## By

## Leondrei Prince

Bloody Money
Bloody Money 2
Me & My Girls

# ...Coming Soon...

The Tommy Good Story

The Rise & Fall of The Capelli Family
And
Frankie 'Lil' Frankie' Maraachi, III

The Tommy Good Story Part II

# Street Knowledge Publishing
## Upcoming Novels

# ..Coming 2007-2008..

**A Day After Forever**
By: Willie Dutch

**Dipped Up**
By: Visa Rollack

**No Love-No Pain**
By: Sicily

**Lust, Love, & Lies**
By: Eric Fleming

**Unlovable Bitch**
By: Allysha Hamber

**The Fold**
By: Tehuti Atum-Ra

**Dopesick 2**
By: Sicily

**NEMESIS**
By: Tehuti Atum-Ra

**White Collar Hustler**
By: Willie Dutch

**Court In The Streets**
By: Kevin Bullock

**Pain Freak**
By: Gregory Garrett

**Playin' For Keeps**
By: Gregory Garrett

**Stackin' Paper**
By: JoeJoe

**The Rise And Fall**
By: Leondrei Prince

**Shakers**
By: Gregory D. Dixon

**A Day After Forever 2**
By: Willie Dutch

**Court In The Streets 2**
By: Kevin Bullock

**The Tommy Good Story**
By: Leondrei Prince

# Street Knowledge Publishing Order Form

Street Knowledge Publishing, P.O. Box 345, Wilmington, DE 19801
Email: jj@streetknowledgepublishing.com
Website: www.streetknowledgepublishing.com

For Inmates Orders and Manuscript Submissions
P.O. Box 310367, Jamaica, NY 11431

*Bloody Money*
ISBN # 0-9746199-0-6                $15.00
Shipping/ Handling Via
U.S. Priority Mail                  $5.25
Total                               $20.25

*Me & My Girls*
ISBN # 0-9746199-1-4                $15.00
Shipping/ Handling Via
U.S. Priority Mail                  $5.25
Total                               $20.25

*Bloody Money 2*
ISBN # 0-9746199-2-2                $15.00
Shipping/ Handling Via
U.S. Priority Mail                  $5.25
Total                               $20.25

*Dopesick*
ISBN # 0-9746199-4-9                $15.00
Shipping/ Handling Via
U.S. Priority Mail                  $5.25
Total                               $20.25

*Money-Grip*
ISBN # 0-9746199-3-0                $15.00
Shipping/ Handling Via
U.S. Priority Mail                  $5.25
Total                               $20.25

*The Queen of New York*
ISBN # 0-9746199-7-3                $15.00
Shipping/ Handling Via
U.S. Priority Mail                  $5.25
Total                               $20.25

*Don't Mix The Bitter With The Sweet*
ISBN # 0-9746199-6-5                $15.00
Shipping/ Handling Via
U.S. Priority Mail                  $5.25
Total                               $20.25

Street Knowledge Publishing, P.O. Box 345, Wilmington, DE 19801
Email: jj@streetknowledgepublishing.com
Website: www.streetknowledgepublishing.com

### The Hunger
ISBN # 0-9746199-5-7      $15.00
Shipping/ Handling Via
U.S. Priority Mail      $5.25
Total      $20.25

### Sin 4 Life
ISBN # 0-9746199-8-1      $15.00
Shipping/ Handling Via
U.S. Priority Mail      $5.25
Total      $20.25

### The Tommy Good Story
ISBN # 0-9799556-0-2      $15.00
Shipping/ Handling Via
U.S. Priority Mail      $5.25
Total      $20.25

### The NorthSide Clit
ISBN # 0-9746199-9-X      $15.00
Shipping/ Handling Via
U.S. Priority Mail      $5.25
Total      $20.25

### Bloody Money III
ISBN # 0-9799556-4-5      $15.00
Shipping/ Handling Via
U.S. Priority Mail      $5.25
Total      $20.25

### Court in the Streets
ISBN # 0-9799556-2-9      $15.00
Shipping/ Handling Via
U.S. Priority Mail      $5.25
Total      $20.25

### A Day After Forever
ISBN # 0-9799556-1-0      $15.00
Shipping/ Handling Via
U.S. Priority Mail      $5.25
Total      $20.25

Street Knowledge Publishing, P.O. Box 345, Wilmington, DE 19801
Email: jj@streetknowledgepublishing.com
Website: www.streetknowledgepublishing.com

### *Dipped Up*
**ISBN # 0-9799556-5-3**          **$15.00**
**Shipping/ Handling Via**
**U.S. Priority Mail**            **$5.25**
**Total**                         **$20.25**

### *Playn' for Keeps*
**ISBN # 0-9799556-9-6**          **$15.00**
**Shipping/ Handling Via**
**U.S. Priority Mail**            **$5.25**
**Total**                         **$20.25**

### *Stackin' Paper*
**ISBN # 0-9755811-1-2**          **$15.00**
**Shipping/ Handling Via**
**U.S. Priority Mail**            **$5.25**
**Total**                         **$20.25**

# Street Knowledge Publishing LLC
## Purchaser Order Form

Date: _____

Purchaser _____

Mailing Address _____

City _____ State _____ Zip Code _____

| Quantity | Title of Book | Price Each | Total |
|---|---|---|---|
| | Bloody Money | $ 15.00 | $ |
| | Bloody Money 2 | 15.00 | |
| | Me & My Girls | 15.00 | |
| | Dopesick | 15.00 | |
| | Money-Grip | 15.00 | |
| | The Queen Of New York | 15.00 | |
| | Don't Mix The Bitter With The Sweet | 15.00 | |
| | Sin 4 Life | 15.00 | |
| | The NorthSide Clit | 15.00 | |
| | The Hunger | 15.00 | |
| | The Tommy Good Story | 15.00 | |
| | Court In The Streets | 15.00 | |
| | Bloody Money III | 15.00 | |
| | Playin' For Keeps | 15.00 | |
| | A Day After Forever | 15.00 | |
| | No Love, No Pain | 15.00 | |
| | Dipped-Up | 15.00 | |
| | Lust, Love & Lies | 15.00 | |
| | | | |
| | | | |
| | | | |
| | | | |
| | Total Books Ordered | Subtotal | |
| | | Shipping | |
| | (Priority Mail $5.25 each) (If ordering more than one add $2.00 each) | | |
| | | Total | $ |

# In Stores Now

STREET KNOWLEDGE PUBLISHING PRESENTS

# Dopesick
THE OTHER SIDE OF THE GAME

A Novel By Sicily

ISBN No. 0-9746199-4-

# ..Coming Soon..

No Love, No Pain
Dopesick 2

# In Stores Now

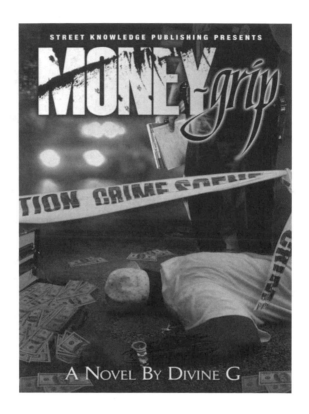

ISBN No. 0-9746199-3-0

# ..Coming Soon..

Money-Grip 2

# In Stores Now

ISBN No. 0-9746199-7-3

# ..Coming Soon..

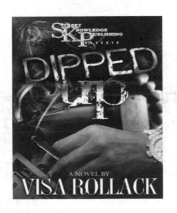

ISBN No.  0-9799556-5-3

# In Stores Now

**ISBN No. 0-9746199-6-5**

# ..Coming Soon..

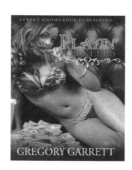

**ISBN No. 0-9799556-9-6**

**ISBN No. 0-9799556-3-7**

# In Stores Now

A Novel By Parish Sherman

**ISBN No. 0-9746199-8-1**

# ..Coming Soon..

A Little Mo' Sin

# In Stores Now

ISBN No. 0-9746199-9-X

# ..Coming Soon..

Unloveable Bitch

# In Stores Now

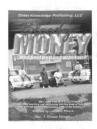

ISBN # 0-9746199-0-6

ISBN # 0-9746199-1-4

ISBN # 0-9746199-2-2

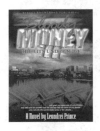

ISBN # 0-9799556-4-5

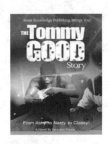

ISBN # 0-9799556-0-2

# ..Coming Soon..

The Rise And Fall
The Tommy Good Story 2

# In Stores Now

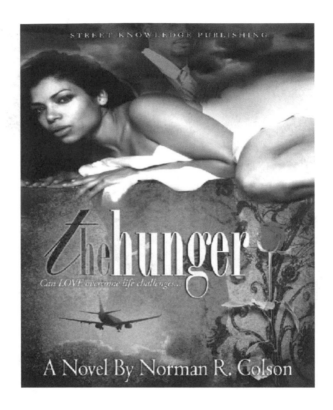

ISBN No. 0-9746199-5-7

# ..Coming Soon..

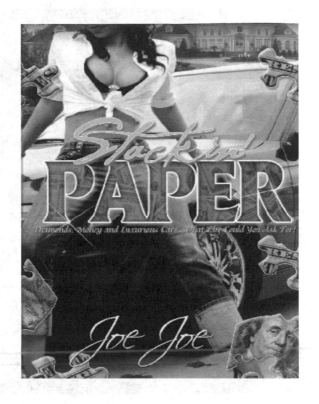

ISBN No. 0-9755811-1-2

# In Stores Now

**ISBN No. 0-9799556-2-9**

# ..Coming Soon..

Court In The Streets Part 2: The Yard

# In Stores Now

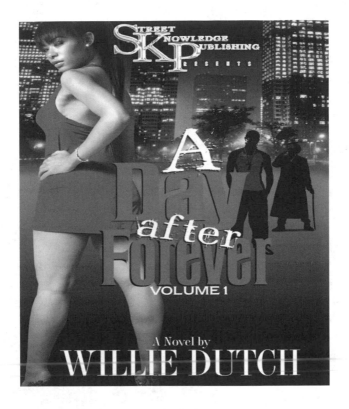

ISBN No. 0-9799556-1-0

# ..Coming Soon..

White Collar Hustler
A Day After Forever 2: The Payback